FRISKY COLLECTIONS VOLUME 1

FRISKY & QUEER

THE FRISKY BEAN
BOOK 1.5

MICHELLE MARS

This collection of stories is dedicated to love. While each one is about finding the right person, the most important love is the love you have for yourself. Just like the characters in these stories, we all deserve that love and no one--by law, judgment, bad relationship, or otherwise--can take it away from you. Love on!

FRISKY RIVALRY

1

HE RUINS EVERYTHING

Tabitha

"WHAT THE HELL are you doing here?" I swear, if Sean Bennet was here to ruin one more thing for me, it was going to be the last day of his existence. Images of exactly how it would play out formed in my head. Coffee in hand, I would leap across the table, tossing the hot liquid ahead of me—so I could distract him—while the rest of me full-body slammed him into oblivion.

I admit, that it might seem a wee bit dramatic, but if anyone understood the nature of our relationship, they would cheer me on.

He tore me out of my oh-so-slightly, over-the-top thoughts when he said in his oh-so-infuriatingly, deep voice, "Tabby Cat, if you wanted to have coffee together, you just had to ask. You didn't have to follow me like a lovesick stalker."

"I wouldn't stalk you if you were the last chocolate bar on earth."

He smirked. "So... you're saying stalking isn't off the table for you then?"

I narrowed my eyes wishing lasers were shooting from my cool grays into his smug, dirt-browns. Okay. They weren't really dirt-brown, more like a rich chestnut, but I would never admit to that. I could play his game, though, and do it better. In a sweetly seductive tone, I replied, "Oh Sean. There's a lot on the table, but none of it will ever concern you."

His smirk got even smirkier, if that's even a thing, and he said, "There's always the counter, the wall, or the bed. In fact, your table couldn't even handle me."

I strained a muscle in my face keeping my expression set to bored indifference when what I felt was anything but. "My table could handle anything you dished out, I just don't invite unworthy people to my dinner parties."

He chortled. He had no right being sexy while chortling, but my insides could never resist turning a bit gooey when we sparred. His ability to respond in kind was an unfortunate turn-on. Why did I have to be so sapiosexual? I like big brains and I cannot lie. It's infuriating.

"It's a party now? Well, this did turn interesting. Just how many people attend your dinner parties?" He leaned forward propping his chiseled chin on one hand. Even his flopping, black hair fell offensively forward over his forehead as though it, too, was waiting for my answer.

Answer I did. I gave him the bird and looked around for an open table as far away from him as possible. The cheery, red-haired owner of the café, Summer, seemed to suddenly find something interesting on a wall having been caught snooping into our display of mutual disdain. I continued with my survey for a table.

Stomping in frustration, well, not really, I would never, but my inner child was rocking the floorboards because the only available table was right next to his sorry ass.

At this point, anyone would be wondering why we have so much animosity between us, well, clearly it was his fault. When we first met in high school, we were both competing for class president. The second time we took notice of each other, we were both wanting first place at the school science fair. From there, we competed for the affection of Ina Gupta, who was too good for either of us; Brad Everly, which was a mistake we both ended up regretting; and Kwon Seong-min, who was done with our competition for them within a couple of days. There were so many instances. For a while, we were sales managers for competing clothing companies and now we've somehow found ourselves working for the same place, Rivalité, a high-end fashion house. In theory, that would put us on the same side, but instead we're competing for the same promotion.

There was only one time where we seemed to be on the same page, but even that went horribly wrong. So here we are, in the same café, having to sit right next to each other, when I'm supposed to be on a blind date I set up through Immedia-date.

This could not be happening to me.

He continued mocking me. "Are you planning to sit down or are you planning to scare off some of the other patrons?"

I ignored his humorous, triumphant smirk and checked out my phone instead. Perhaps there was still time to redirect my date so we could meet somewhere else. The Frisky Bean was my favorite, but I was willing to compromise if I could have my date in peace.

Nope. My bad luck was holding because the app said Felix was nearby.

There was nothing left for it, I sat down nearly shoulder-to-shoulder with my arch nemesis. *Fuck my life.*

2

SHE RUINS EVERYTHING

Sean

WHAT WAS SHE DOING HERE? She was going to ruin everything. She always ruined everything for me. There is too much history to go into, but from the moment that Tabitha Chase entered my life, she had me scrambling to stay ahead—or keep up—depending on which situation we were discussing. A literal thorn in my side would be more comfortable. The worst part of it all was my infernal attraction to her.

Why her? Why couldn't my libido find anyone else to focus on? I mean, of course over the years I've focused on other people, some of the time. I've taken no vows of celibacy. But, those attractions were always fleeting while the one I've had for her lingers like a skunk scent and is just as irritating. It's especially perplexing since I already know that it would never be good between us.

It makes absolutely no sense.

And here she is, once again, about to ruin my blind date. It will be quite difficult to focus my attention on someone new while my

6

body is still trying to make an undesired connection. I'd try to divert my date to a new location but a part of me is stubborn enough, competitive enough, and probably childish enough to decide I'd been here first and I was not going to be the one that needs to move.

Instead... I prodded the bear for my amusement. "So... what brings you to this café for lunch today and are you sure you wouldn't be more comfortable doing anything else at any other location?"

Her eye roll had to hurt it was so intense. "I'm meeting someone. Why don't you take your drink with you as you survey the plethora of other locations you can darken with your personality." And, there was the viper-tongued Tabby I knew and loathed.

Since my date hadn't yet arrived, I kept pushing her.

I was bored.

Sue me.

"Tabby Cat, you're taking note of my personality now? Next thing you know you'll be singing sonnets about me."

"I don't sing but I'm happy to dump this coffee on your head for an interactive art exhibit I'm calling, 'Here sits the asshole covered in coffee.' I think it will be a hit. You?"

I couldn't help it. I laughed. Her quick-witted responses were so unpredictable. I looked out the window of the café and spotted my date taking a phone call. "Ah. There's my date now."

"I hadn't heard you were seeing anyone," she said as she followed my gaze.

"I'm not. It's a blind date, but very promising based on our profiles."

I noticed she tensed and then shook her head in what seemed amusement. "Of course you're here on a blind date. How very *us* this is. I'm meeting a blind date as well."

"What interesting timing. Are they here yet?" I looked out the window again. My date was going to be late soon, but was still chatting away on their phone.

Tabby scanned out the window and shook her head. "Not yet."

I prodded once again, because of course I had to. "Perhaps they're standing you up."

Her hands clawed on the table. "Felix isn't standing me up. The app says she's nearby. Anyway, it doesn't look like your date is anxious to meet you. They're quite into that conversation they're having."

She was not wrong, which irked me, so I tightened my grip on my coffee but kept my tone light as I responded, "And yet they, at least, are here."

"You arrogant assho—"

Her words dropped off abruptly so I looked to where she was looking. Outside the café a person with short blue hair wandered up to my date. They appeared to know each other and my date got off of their call to chat. Their conversation only lasted a minute but then both got their phones out and started texting before walking away together.

At that moment, both our phones beeped. I looked down at the notification from Immedia-date letting me know that my date apologized but they won't be able to make it.

In unison, Tabby and I said, "Crap."

3

LEFT BEHIND

Tabby

"I THINK my date just absconded with *your* date." I can't believe this is happening! How did the timing of all this land exactly so that I was left sitting here with Sean. It's like that romance-book-reasons bull-shit that my book club jokes about. Yet here we are.

He grimaced, "I think you may be right." He dropped his phone back to the table and the movement had me looking at his hand. It was a strong hand. With corded veins leading to forearms that were visible because he had the audacity to roll up his shirt sleeves.

The universe was a cruel, cruel place.

"Are you checking out my arms, Tabby Cat?"

I startled at his question and nearly choked on the sip of coffee I'd taken to quench the thirst I'd developed. In between coughs, I splut-tered, "Of course not! I was just wondering if your date gave you any more details as to why they wandered off together. Mine said that she ran into an old friend. Was wondering if that was code for ex-partner."

He didn't answer me right away and instead watched me in a way that made me feel all hot and bothered again. *What the hell? This is so out of control. He's your enemy you dolt. Get your shit together and stop finding him hot already.* I may have squirmed in my seat. Just a little. I think I successfully covered it up though with the lingering coughs.

"Are you sure you weren't checking out my arms? You seem a bit squirmy, Tabby Cat." Dammit. Guess he noticed. Not only that, but for some reason Sean leaned in closer when he spoke and I could practically feel his breath on my neck.

Defense! Quick! "Stop calling me that ridiculous name and if you don't mind staying at your table instead of practically crawling into my lap, I'd appreciate it."

"You sure you don't want me in your lap?"

Imagining all five-foot-ten of him on my five-foot-three lap broke whatever hold he had on me and I laughed. The absurdity was too much. The tension between us released as he laughed too.

"I can't believe you asked me that. You're ridiculous."

"Maybe so." He paused, grew contemplative. "But, you can't tell me you don't still feel the attraction between us, can you?" His hand reached out and gently covered my own as it sat on my thigh.

Oh my. Like those nineties-style leggings with foot-straps, the sexual tension came back around... unwanted. I may have needed a breath or two before getting a hold of myself and replying. "Of course I feel it, I'm not completely unaware. I just don't understand it. You want to tell me you do?"

He appeared to be choosing his words quite carefully. "I can't say that I completely understand it myself after..." He just left it dangling there and we both could fill in the blanks. After last time. After the one time we gave in.

"Yes... after. Exactly."

"It has been three years since..." Once again, he just left all the things unsaid. They didn't need saying. We both knew what happened even if we tried to play it off.

It was time to clear that elephant out of the room. After so many years, we needed to be adults about this. "Since we had the worst one-night stand in the history of one-night stands?"

He visibly cringed at my description but we both knew I wasn't wrong.

Three years ago we gave in to our desire. We were at the same conference and after years of banter and lusting, we fell into each other. It should have been amazing. It should have been the hottest night of our lives. In romance stories, this is where we would have orgasmed in such concordance that our souls would have vibrated in perfect harmony or something. That was *not* what happened. In fact, I wasn't exaggerating how bad it was. I didn't get off and when he went to dispose of the condom, I swiftly got dressed and called out a quick thanks before he returned. I went to my hotel room and got myself off instead. We never spoke of it again.

That's why it's so confusing that we still have sexual tension between us. It makes no sense. We tried. It was horrible. So why do I still want him?

4

———————————————————————

THE NIGHT WE DON'T TALK ABOUT

Sean

OUCH! I wish I could say Tabby was wrong, but what probably hurts the most is that she isn't. What a horrible night. I didn't even come. I actually had to pretend to come which, come on, you hear of women faking it, which they absolutely shouldn't have to, but men? Yeah. That was me that night, faking it. I then ran to "dispose of the condom" but instead was staring at myself in the mirror in confusion when she called that she was leaving and, thank god for small miracles because I was able to rub one out once she was gone.

What has never been gone is my desire for this woman. It's the height of idiocy to continue to pursue something with someone after the night we shared but here we were. Apparently, I was a total glutton for punishment and wanted to try again.

"I know we didn't make the last time very good."

She scoffed. "Not very good?"

We were both momentarily distracted from our conversation as someone near us got up from their table giving us some curious looks as they left. Apparently, while we were engrossed in our conversation, a few of the tables around us had emptied. Summer, the friendly barista, was standing there cleaning one table over and over again. When she saw she'd been caught, she shuffled off with an apologetic expression, but not before knocking into the table she had been shining to a gleam.

Tabby leaned closer to hiss, "What we experienced in that hotel room was more than not very good. Be honest Sean."

Ignoring the heat building in me from her nearness, I lowered my tone to match hers and whispered, "Okay. It was markedly bad. I don't think I've ever not come with someone before."

She gasped and her cheeks flamed. "You didn't come? You sounded like you were coming! Are you telling me you faked it?"

"Are you telling me you didn't?"

That made her pause because we both knew she had and we didn't believe in double standards. "Fair point. But, it only makes the argument against us ever acting on whatever this is stronger."

Even as she was denying us, I caught her glancing at my lips like she wanted a bite. "The pull is so strong though. Maybe we've gotten older and have grown out of whatever happened the last time. I think it's worth considering."

"Even if that were true. We work together. We are competing for a promotion. This is not a good idea and you know it. That's not even touching on how much I loathe you." A small smile played on her lips. We both said those things, but I don't think either of us ever truly loathed the other. Well, since adulthood, anyway. There was definitely some loathing going on when we competed for class president.

"We can continue to throw all sorts of obstacles in our way, sure. And, I would never pressure you to doing anything you didn't want." I don't think she took notice of the fact that she was still leaning into me or that I was still holding her hand on her leg.

"Why do I hear a 'but' already?"

"Probably because there is one. You see, all those things are true, *but* I still want nothing more in this moment than to lean over and kiss you. No… Devour you. I'm practically feral inside." We were so close I could pick up on the subtle changes as her breath caught and her heart started racing. She licked her lips and I couldn't drag my eyes from the sight.

"Fine. Then kiss me. It will probably be equally as ba—"

I wasn't going to let her finish that sentence and she had given me permission, so… I kissed her. It started with pressing my lips to hers but pretty soon, I forgot where we were and I was delving my tongue between her lips, mingling the taste of my sweeter caramel macchiato with her darker, deeper flavored French kiss coffee. We tasted good together. I was lost in the decadence of our kiss for some unknown amount of time until a crash from behind the counter had me coming up for air.

Tabby looked as dazed as I felt. "That was far, far from bad."

Her face scrunched up in horror or disappointment, not sure which and she said, "Really? You kiss me like that and your declaration afterward is 'far from bad?' Way to make a girl feel special, jackass."

Tabby was not wrong. If I handled my pitches like I handled that after-kiss discourse, I'd be out of a job. *Get your head back in the game before you lose her interest.* "I fumbled that. What I meant to say was that the kiss should be proof that maybe things would be different today versus back then because it was a truly inspired kiss. No other kiss could possibly compare."

She visibly relaxed and, what else was promising, was that she hadn't leaned back away from me. We were still intimately close. "Better. I'm convinced. Were you planning to go back into the office after this, attend a client meeting, or were you heading home for some work-from-home hours?"

One of the things I always appreciated about Tabby was that she was quick to assess a situation and then made swift decisions. She followed her instincts so easily while I enjoyed working out the best solution to things with lists, charts, and a lack of spontaneity. That was one of the reasons I loved to compete with her. She made me a more agile thinker.

That came in useful in that moment because I'd had every intention of going back to the office, but instead answered, "The last option. I was planning to work-from-home. How about you? Are you joining me?"

5

———————————————

"WORKING" FROM HOME

Tabby

"ME TOO. And... yes, I'll join you." What was I saying? I had planned to do my quickie lunch date and then head back to work. I was going to have to call my assistant and make sure she knew I wasn't coming back today. All this because of a freaking kiss. It better be good this time, because I definitely was not interested in rearranging my day just for terrible sex. That kiss though...

A sultry grin had shown up on his face when I agreed to join him and it was infectious. I could feel my matching grin taking shape.

"Shall we get out of here?"

"Yes. But..."

"But?"

"I want to take some pinch me poached pear pockets with us. If we succeed in making it good, then I plan to work up an appetite and those things are divine." I waggled my eyebrows at Sean. I really do love this café. I'm here so many times a week, I should be earning frequent flier miles.

16

"That sounds like an excellent plan to me." Together we bought the tasty treats and while Summer looked like she could be the first gif in a search of "inquiring minds want to know" she kept her questions to herself. I was sure she'd be drilling me about it when I came in later in the week for Frisky Book Club, though.

I wasn't keen on leaving my car, and for work reasons, I knew Sean's address so after another noteworthy kiss that had me making lists of the wicked things I wanted to do with him, we got into our separate vehicles and drove to his condo. I had just enough time to contact my assistant to switch my schedule to be "working-from-home" for the rest of the day. It was also just enough time for me to start second guessing our decision. I was not interested in a repeat of our previous night together. No, thank you. Mistakes were meant to be learned from not repeated.

When I arrived, I was lucky to find a guest spot open near the door into the building. I figured I'd have to meet him inside since his parking would be in a different location. Just enough time alone to give me even more second thoughts. *Perfect.*

It was a good thing he opened the door when he entered but hadn't shut it, because I had nearly convinced myself to turn right back and leave. With the door open, he saw me as soon as I walked up and at a speed I didn't know he possessed, he had me inside, door closed, and testing how sturdy a door it was. My back can confirm it's quite strong, pressed so firmly against it as I was.

His lips were liquid fire as he kissed me, burning away all doubts and leaving nothing but hot desire behind. Minutes went by lost in our kiss. Eventually, I needed to come up for air so I broke it off panting. Gasping. "Do you greet everyone who walks in front of your door this way? It's effective."

"No. Only stray Tabby Cats get this kind of attention."

He didn't just say that. "You didn't just say that." I cracked up laughing so hard he had to back away and give me some space. "That was so damn cheesy." *I mean. It was.* It wasn't at all that he had been looking so deeply into my eyes that I started to panic from the strength of whatever this was between us. Nope. Not at all. "I'm sorry. That just struck my funny bone. I'll compose myself. Where were we?"

His feelings in the brief amount of time I'd been laughing like a loon, scrolled swiftly across his face from a little hurt, to annoyance, to amusement, and circling back around to heat as I advanced on him, grabbing him by the belt, yanking him to me, and smashing my mouth back to his aggressively. I little too aggressively, it seemed, as our teeth clinked against each other. I was about to pull back again from sheer embarrassment but his hand wove into my hair at the back of my neck keeping me in place for him to once again deepen our kiss most evocatively.

I began walking towards him, causing him to walk backwards until we reached his couch. He fell backwards taking a seat which I hadn't calculated accurately since his hand was still tangled in my hair. His sudden drop pulled my head down directly into his crotch. Missed it by a mere inch to the left and I got a face of thigh instead.

"Are you okay?" We both said in unison.

He let go of my head and I sat down next to him with a huff. "What is wrong with us? This is turning into just as bad of a disaster as the last time."

"I really don't want to agree with you and for sure my dick doesn't want me to, but yeah, something isn't clicking when it should be. I want you so much."

"I want you too... but not like this. If we could make it feel as good as my desire for you, I'd be down for a wake the neighbors all-nighter."

We sat side-by-side staring at the walls like they would suddenly form words of advice. Of course, if they had, I would have been out of his apartment and getting ready to torch the place. I'd seen enough horror movies to know that writing on the wall was always a bad sign. There was no writing, but I did have an epiphany upon reflection.

"I think I may have an idea about our problem. Are you willing to experiment with me?"

He looked over by rolling his head on the back of the couch to face me. "Sure. I'm open to all suggestions that allow me to go down this road with you and actually arrive at mutual orgasms."

"I... I think that we are so used to competing with each other that we don't know how to stop." I nervously looked to see what his reaction to that was, but he seemed to be listening intently. His face lacked any opinion one way or another. So, I continued, "From my end, I'm realizing that I've been trying to one up you on who is 'in-charge,' trying to prove I'm a lusty monster, pushing to show you just how sexy I am, racing you to the finish line—though we both know now, that neither of us did—and so many other examples if I spent even more time evaluating our interactions then and now." I thought I was onto something and anxiously waited to see if he agreed with me.

He was pensive and why was that so, so sexy?

Ugh.

6

EXPERIMENTATION

Sean

WAS SHE RIGHT? Was competing their problem all along? I didn't want to rush to judgment because I didn't want to mess things up. We were giving it another shot and unbeknownst to Tabby, I'd been waiting for this day. I thought we'd never get another chance after the-day-that-no-one-came. If she and I could ever get on the same page, I knew we could be an unstoppable team. Looking back at our interactions, I had to admit she had a point and that gave me an idea. I looked into her gray worried eyes and gave her a lopsided smile.

"I think you are on to something. What is your experiment?"

She took a breath that seemed to help her shoulders detach from around her ears. "I suggest we take turns being in charge. Perhaps if it is assigned we can stop trying to outdo each other."

"If I may propose, are you open to a similar experiment? Instead of being assigned a role, we focus on pleasure." I snaked my arm around her middle, turning her body fully toward mine. "Each other's pleasure to be exact. Let go of everything else and sink into feeling. All I want is to make you scream my name as you come all over my mouth, my fingers, or my cock. I think that sounds pretty win-win, don't you?"

Her pupils were completely blown with lust by the time I stopped talking. With her legs on either side of my hips, I finished laying out my counter-point. "What do you say, Tabby Cat? May I give you pleasure?"

She nodded, her breathing ragged. "Fuck me, Sean. You've given me a list of your deliverables and I want every last one." She wrapped her hand around my neck and drew me into a deep, sensual kiss as she lay back, bringing me with her.

My hard length was nestled in her wet heat, noticeable despite the clothes between us. This time, we would go slower. More exploration, than invasion. More intense, than frenzied. The fire was still there, but we were sharing in it instead of hurling fireballs at each other. In quick work, I had her pants off and her shirt unbuttoned. Her black lace bra delicately hugged her perfect tits. Gorgeous. I kissed my way down the parted halves of her shirt until I reached the lace and closed my mouth around one firm peak moistening the lace as I sucked. Tabby moaned and ran her hand through my hair in reaction.

I did the same to the other one but sucked harder and her fingers twitched grasping the strands of my hair for a moment as she gasped. I worshiped them both, collecting her reactions like little trophies. First with the lace, but eventually, I pushed the cups down and enjoyed the taste of her in my mouth. Her skin was flushed and hot. Splotches of deep red across her olive-toned skin like a trail I was happy to follow to her light tan nipples.

Eventually, I decided to wander further down the trail. Kissing and licking my way down her soft belly over her curls and finally landing at the juncture of her thick thighs. Kneeling on the floor between her legs, I tasted every inch of her making sure to pay equal attention to her left and right labia. I'd heard somewhere that women couldn't figure out why men always favored the left one and missed the clitoris entirely. After hearing that, I'd vowed to never be that man, so after giving both sides the attention they deserved, I went for the bean at her core like a hungry man.

And I *was* hungry. I'd been starving to find a way to connect with this woman for *way* too long. We finally seemed to be on the same page. My cock was absolutely certain of it and wasn't sure why he was still in solitary but I'd get to him soon enough. I was enjoying making Tabby purr for me too much to stop. "Come for me Tabby Cat. Give me what I want and I'll declare you the winner."

"I don't need your declarations, I just need your mouth getting back to work. You feel so good. So good, Sean."

"As you say. Would you like to put my fingers to work too?" She nodded emphatically and a split second later two of my fingers entered her as she squirmed, bucking her hips. I went back to work with my mouth and within a minute, her insides tensed around me as she came with a shudder. As she was coming down, I licked at the evidence of her pleasure lingering on my fingers after I pulled them out. "You are absolutely delicious."

Our eyes met and hers were a bit unfocused. Job well done, if I say so myself.

7

YOU LOOKED LIKE MINE

Tabby

HOLY SHIT. That was... fantastic. I'd just had the best orgasm with a man that I'd ever had in my life and it was with Sean? Well, I was downright excited. So much so that I promptly lost all game and yelled, "Woohoo! We did it!" and then offered him a high-five.

For his part, Sean sat up and high-fived me right back chuckling. "I've never had a reason to high-five my partner after sex before but I appreciate the direct feedback for my performance evaluation. Efficient and conveys the message rather well."

"I can't believe I did that. I'm sorry." I was so freaking embarrassed. What's wrong with me? A high-five? Really? But... What the hell. I decided to lean into it. "Of course, if you play your cards right, you might just get a gold star the next time or even two thumbs up."

"I can only aspire."

He stood up following that statement, and I couldn't help but notice the bulge tenting his pants so of course I pointed at it. "That looks... uncomfortable."

"It is. I think my cock is about to file a complaint for favoritism in the workplace."

I wrapped my fingers around him over his clothes, leaned over, and pretended to be speaking directly into the "microphone." "Ladies and gentlepeople, prepare for things to take a turn in a more stiff direction. Try not to gag or get choked up at what you experience." He was chuckling as he placed one knee on the couch looming above where I now sat, but as I undid his pants and eased his dick out of his boxer briefs, his breath caught when my lips made kiss contact with the head.

My voice came out husky as I said, "My turn," before taking him into my mouth fully. He let out a grunt followed by a moan and I began to work him. His hand tangled in my short curls. I treated him like my favorite dessert and was treated in return with filthy words and sounds spilling from his mouth. Eventually, I decided I wasn't getting the leverage and control I wanted in our positions so I stopped long enough to push him to a sitting position on the couch, legs splayed, one on the couch and one on the floor. I laid belly down on the pillows and found the angle I wanted with my head between those powerful thighs. I licked him from balls to tip.

"That's better."

"I'll sit in whatever way you want to get your mouth on me again. Pretzel me if it suits you but give me that wicked tongue and sensuous mouth. Please."

"Begging. I like it." And I did. In fact, I was so fond of it, that I chose to surprise him and took him into my mouth as deep as I could on the first reentry. I wrapped one hand around the base to keep me from going too deep and then swiftly got back into a rhythm. I noted what area was most sensitive to him and revisited it with my tongue and lips. For his part, he was staring down at me with lust and appreciation clear as day in his expression. The power of it was heady.

So much so, that I found my hips were pumping into the couch in sync with my mouth. My breasts were also stimulated by the combined softness of the couch and the roughness of the lace. I was getting close to coming again simply by watching this man I'd been hungering for, slowly come apart. He was so beautiful. His breaths grew more ragged and soon he said, "I'm going to come, if you don't want it down your throat, you need to stop.

I was not stopping. I wanted it. I wanted him. I sucked harder and a couple of passes later, he came and I swallowed him down.

"Well damn, Tabby Cat... that was quite the sight."

"Let me guess." I chuckled as I sat up. "I looked good with your cock in my mouth?"

"You did, but not what I was going to say."

"Then what were you about to say?"

"I don't think I'm going to tell you what I thought just yet." He joked as he ruffled some of my curls.

"A mystery. How intriguing." That's what I *said*, but I was patting my mouth as I faked a yawn while saying it. "I think our little experiment worked. Don't you?"

"I *think* we've only collected partial data and while it is a promising start, we should make sure to run the full experiment before coming to any conclusions." He didn't even give me the time to fully process his points before he had me over his shoulder staring at his butt while walking down the hall and into his bedroom.

"You heavy-handed jackass, let me down." I truly attempted to keep a cool expression and tone, but all of it came out between giggles and wailing.

"Never say I don't do anything for you." He plopped me down on his bed with a bounce and I rolled with my laughter. "Laugh now, get it out, because soon you'll be screaming my name as originally promised."

"Will I?" I attempted to roll off of the bed and onto my feet, ready to run when his arm caught me around the waist.

He pulled me in tight, my back to his front and surprisingly he appeared to be in the first stages of getting hard again already. His voice dripped sex appeal as he whispered in my ear, "Caught."

So it seemed. "What do you plan to do with me now?"

"I want you completely naked. I want to also be nude and I want to make love to you, I want to fill you, I still want you screaming my name. I want to make you feel really fucking good. Lastly, baby..." He paused.

The silence was too much for me. "Yes?"

"Lastly..." He paused again and began nuzzling my neck.

"Lastly, what? Just spit it out already." Goosebumps rose along my arms as he licked a path along the side and then gently blew on it. The rapid cool was a wicked sensation.

"Lastly, I want to see if I can earn those two thumbs up."

Okay. I freely admit with him playing with one of my personal erogenous zones so completely, it took a second or two for me to figure out what he was saying. I grouched back jokingly this time, unlike earlier, "Have I mentioned how much I loathe you?"

"It's come up a time or two."

There wasn't much talking after that as he peeled all my clothes from me, I did the same with his, and together we matched our bodies on the bed. From his slight belly, to his strong shoulders, from his bubble butt, to his nearly bare pecs, I enjoyed every piece of him. Explored every piece of him. Things felt so right this time compared to that time-that-shall-not-be-named.

By the time he reached over to the nightstand to grab a condom, I had come one more time with his hand and kisses. I was so ready for him. He even did the romance novel thing where he ripped the wrapper open with his teeth. The books might object that I could wrap my hand around his cock, but I wasn't looking for a tree trunk and something told me, he knew how to use it just fine. I was full of anticipation and longing.

"You look like a nymph sprawled on my bed in sexual abandon. It's now my favorite image." He rolled the condom onto his length and came back into the circle of my arms aligning our bodies perfectly.

I wrapped my legs around his hips and as he leaned down to

whisper something in my ear, he thrust home and left me gasping for two reasons.

He whispered, "What I was going to say earlier... was that you looked like mine."

8

―――――――――

NO REGRETS

Sean

THIS WOMAN HAS BEEN a part of my life for so long—a part of me really—and we were finally getting it right. She felt incredible. I couldn't remember a time I was this attuned to another person. She got me in ways no one else ever had. It was the very reason we were always at each other. Two peas in a pod needing to figure out how to be together.

We were together now and it was better than I could have imagined after the disaster of before. We'd found our alignment.

"Sean," she panted.

"Yes, Tabby?"

Her claws, I mean nails, bit into my shoulders as she bucked her hips, sinking me deeper. "I'll experiment with you any day, but do you think you could conclude this round sooner than later?"

My thoughts exactly. "Play with your clit for me. I'll handle the rest." She did just that. Her hand wove between our bodies, after she sucked two of her fingers into her mouth, and began circling it in earnest. "Come for me, baby."

I ratcheted up my pace watching as Tabby fell apart for me gasp by gasp. A sensual goddess. I kissed the gasps from her mouth and squeezed her breast when she seemed close. "Oh! I... Sean!"

With my name on her lips, her body convulsed as she came, soaking my cock, and I couldn't hold on any longer. "Tabby. Fuuuck."

I was spent, but I kept kissing her face, shoulders, lips, basically, anywhere my mouth could reach until finally settling my forehead to hers. I stayed like that as our breathing slowed and the world around us came back into focus. "I have to get rid of the condom, but don't you move."

"I'm not going anywhere. My body is Jell-O-ish right now."

I gave her one last kiss on the nose as I got up to do what I said. On the way back, I brought a warm washcloth and carefully cleaned Tabby. The silence as I worked was unusual for us, but not uncomfortable. We were both seemingly lost to our afterglow. And, it would have been a perfect moment except for one thing. Tabby had never responded to my revelation that she looked like mine.

"Hey... Sean?" Her voice was post-sexually husky.

"Yes, Tabby Cat?" I threw the cloth in my hamper and laid down next to her gliding my fingers across her clavicles and then down her sternum. Tracing all of her with gentle caresses.

She pushed me onto my back with a shove to my shoulder before I knew what she was planning. With an unexpected swiftness, considering how boneless she had seemed, she was up and straddling my hips.

"You look like mine too." And that was it. The moment I knew I never wanted to let her go. It took too many years for us to reach this point. To stop competing long enough to reach each other.

"I really, really am."

"And, do you know what I do with what's mine?" she sounded so seductive and sure and I couldn't wait to find out what else she had planned. Though, truth be told, I wasn't sure if I had another round in me right away. I could always stick to my mouth and fingers... I would make it work.

She began tickling me. "You're going to regret this," I said in spurts because I was damn ticklish and she was relentless at finding every spot.

At least, until I grabbed both her wrists and placed her hands above my head causing her face to be just in front of mine. I took her lips in a slow, exploratory kiss. Eventually, we stopped kissing and were left cuddling.

I could practically feel her smirk as she said, "I regret nothing."

9

ANOTHER BLIND DATE

Tabby

A MONTH HAD PASSED since I tripped and fell on Sean's cock. There were challenges we had to overcome like working together, which we were no longer doing because I got a job that was equivalent to the promotion we were both gunning for. Sean was about to get that promotion, but you know, I got there first.

Anyway, we were meeting for a snack date where it all started. I looked into the window of The Frisky Bean and spotted him sitting at our table. He was obviously looking for me too. Our eyes met. The heat that rose in me was in his eyes. A month later and one look could still send the sweetest coiling tension to my insides.

I briefly stopped to greet Summer as I walked in and then made my way to the table. "Excuse me, I'm supposed to meet someone named Sean for a blind date. Are you him?"

The sexy smirk that crossed his face was everything. "It just so happens, it's my lucky day. I am definitely him."

I continued the game I started since he, too, was game. "Oh good. I was worried I might have been stood up."

"Not a chance. I had a feeling about you."

"Did you?" I was momentarily distracted by his hand caressing the side of his coffee like one might a lover.

"Why don't you join me since we're both in the right place with the right person."

He waved his hand at the seat across from him and it jarred me out of my trance picturing him caressing me with those fingers. I sat and stared at the drink in front of me. "You already grabbed me something to drink? That feels rather presumptuous, don't you think? For a blind date, that is."

I was in the process of lifting my cup up to taste, when he responded with, "Of course, but I think I have you nailed."

I spluttered at his word play and was lucky I wasn't spitting anything across the table. "Hmm..." I finally took that sip once I stopped coughing. "Dark and slightly bitter. Pretty much describes my soul, but not the drink I would want right now."

He looked like he didn't believe me. "Are you sure?"

"Quite sure. Do you think I'm just screwing you, I mean, with you?"

"I think this is quickly turning into one of my favorite dates. What do you think, Tabby Cat? Do you mind if I call you Tabby Cat?" He smirked. "Of course not. So... Tabby Cat, are you looking for some cream? In your coffee, of course." I'd grown so fond of that cocky, smug smirk of his.

"No. You may not call me Tabby Cat. It's rather ridiculous to start handing out nicknames when we've just met, right Stud Muffin?"

He abruptly stood up and leaned down whispering directly in my ear, which as always, had a sensual ripple effect down my body. "Don't move."

I wasn't thinking to go anywhere, but that commanding tone, which would have had me wanting to gouge out his eyes last month, had me wanting to sit in anticipation of what he had planned. I didn't have to wait for long. I could sense his presence over my shoulder before feeling his breath at my ear again. His arm reached around to place something on the table even as he said, "One Cinnamon Stud Muffin coming up. I am full service..." he paused dramatically, "Tabby Cat."

My heart which had picked up pace when we first started bantering, then began sprinting in anticipation of what he was planning, was now galloping in longing. Not for the muffin, of course, though it looked damn good, but because I was ready to knock everything off the table and give everyone a show, I was so turned on. And yet, you could take the anger and frustration out of the girl, but you can't take her need to win that easily.

In a voice I hardened to sound firm despite the lust, "Much like this muffin, I could easily devour you. I'm unconvinced you could handle what I'm bringing to the table."

He sat down again facing me with an amused look, letting me know exactly how much gravity he was giving my assessment of the situation. "I'm sure I could handle anything you throw at me. I'll just flip it, wrestle it, and tie it down. I like coming out on top."

I couldn't keep up the pretense after that. I snort laughed so hard. "You know you're still an arrogant ass and I loathe you."

"You're compliments always do wonders for my confidence, love." His hand reached across the table and cupped my face which had my laughter come to an abrupt standstill. "I love you." His eyes were full of his sincerity.

I was barely able to breathe through all my feels. "I love you, too."

He lips quirked and he winked playfully, "If you really want to be on top that bad, I'm willing to bargain."

"You know what I want to bargain about?" I asked oh so sensually.

"What?" he leered.

"The account you are trying to steal from my company. You thought I hadn't noticed?"

His hand dropped from my face and he sat back with another smirk. "Of course I assumed you would notice. It wouldn't be nearly as much fun if you hadn't. But, we have a rule."

He had a point. "I suppose we do."

"Fireworks for our relationship and bazookas for our work. Which explosion are you really wanting right now?"

"Fine. I concede this one. Meet me at our place in ten minutes or I may just start without you. Bye!" With that gauntlet thrown, I swiped my coffee and muffin and ran out of the café before he could respond. One thing our relationship would never be is boring.

10

NORTH STAR

Sean

TABBY THOUGHT she'd pulled a fast one on me rushing out like that, but she was only walking into my trap. I was barely a few steps behind her as she ran out. It was a race to see who got home first, but I was confident knowing our driving styles and based on where I'd ensured I parked, that I'd be the victor.

When I reached home, I swiftly hit play on the music I'd planned, threw my keys to the side, rolled up my sleeves—I knew how much she liked my forearms and so why not—and in one fluid motion, pulled out the box and dropped down on one knee just as the door opened. The look on Tabby's face was priceless. Disbelief that I'd beat her home. Shock at everything from the chilled champagne on our coffee table, to the tulips—her favorite flower—in vases all over the apartment, to me on one knee.

She took a moment to compose herself, closed the door, and slowly strolled over to where I was kneeling. *What was she up to?*

"You cheated."

For a moment I was concerned she took all this to mean I was covering up for having cheated on her—which of course, I would never—but then I saw her lip twitch and the mischievous gleam in her eyes and realized what she meant.

She continued, "From the looks of this place, you knew we'd end up here today and that you would beat me here, which means that you cheated."

"Guilty as charged. To keep up with you, I have to resort to underhanded measures. I apologize for nothing. But, if you don't mind, I'm in the middle of trying to propose to you, so please take your position and let me get on with the matter." I pointed at the "X" that I'd marked on the ground with some tape.

"How specific of you." She stood on the X and I finally saw her underlying emotions as her eyes glistened.

"Tabby Cat, Tabby for short, you have been my rival, my worst one-night stand, my competition, and my thorn." I stopped to clear my throat as I was starting to get a bit choked up too.

Tabby, meanwhile, was giving me her less than amused face. It may have been a bad time to pause so I rushed on.

"You have also been my inspiration, my reason to challenge myself to do and be better, my best night of my life, and the reason I smile. It may be that we have only been together for a month and living together for a couple of weeks, but I can't remember a time when you weren't one of the most profound things in my life and I know that will always hold true. I want you to be the thorn in my side and by my side for the rest of my life. Will you marry me?"

I reached out and held her left hand in anticipation of her answer. I hadn't realized how anxious I would be. I kind of assumed my natural cockiness would carry me through this proposal like a breeze. Instead, I was genuinely concerned that I was doing this too soon. What was probably a few seconds but felt like hours, ended when she said, "Yes."

She sat herself down on my raised thigh and hugged me. "Of course I'll marry you. I can't think of a better way to spend the rest of my life than to challenge you, support you, and torture you—and have you do the same for me. I love you.”

She leaned back and I took the opportunity to slide my ring on her finger. It was a solitary gray star sapphire in a delicate platinum setting. “This reminded me of your eyes and the fact that you have always and will always be the star that is my True North. I hope you like it.” Once again I was struck at the nervousness I was experiencing waiting to hear what she thought. Most people would discuss the engagement ring beforehand but I went with my gut. I hoped it was the right call.

She studied it for only a moment and said, “I absolutely love it.” She threw her arms around me but not before I got a glimpse of the happy tears forming in her eyes. “How dare you make me cry?” she whined.

“I am a right bastard, aren’t I? Don’t think I missed the part where you just vowed to be mine. All mine.” I squeezed her tight as our love for each other filled the room.

A little bit later, obviously having recovered her composure, Tabby reached behind her and brought my hands to her front where she held them. “Some might say this is quick, but we know that isn’t the case at all. Some might say our wedding happened quickly because you know I’m not going to want a long engagement. But, really, I’m just decisive.”

She leaned over, gave me a swift kiss on the lips, and then took off running all the while yelling behind her, “I’ll be starting without you if you don’t hurry up! This is one sexy ring! We need some time together.”

I would have been after her in a flash, but I was knocked over by the speed with which she vacated my leg. I lay there chuckling to myself waiting to hear what she had to say when she saw the surprises I left in the bedroom. Her squeal of delight followed by, “Is this for me to use on you or you to use on me?” was everything I hoped for.

I slowly made my way to the bedroom and leaned on the doorway with my hands in my pockets. Seeing which of the items she was holding I grinned, "Both."

Her eyes grew round and then she jutted one belligerent hip out with a hand on it. "How dare you, sir?"

"How dare I what, Tabby Cat?"

"How dare you have your forearms showing while doing the doorway lean? Seriously, I'm not made of stone."

I crooked a finger and said, "Come here." Step by slow step we came together in the middle. "I adore you."

She quipped, "I loathe you."

"Of course you do."

We kissed until words were no longer necessary.

It was just me.

It was just her.

It was just us.

Tomorrow, we could settle who got the client we were fighting over.

Tonight, we had a different type of entanglement to sort out.

FRISKY ARRANGEMENT

1

———————————————

WRONG IMPRESSIONS

Ash

"ALEXANDRE DESJARDINS?" I inquired about the person kneeling behind the register. It was hard to tell if they were an employee or if they were the owner I was looking for. From what I could see over the counter, they seemed young: floppy, curly light-brown hair cut short on the sides but left longer on top, wrinkle-free pale skin, along with sweet guileless blue eyes that looked up at me, acknowledging my question.

"Yes. That's me. You can call me Alex, they, them. Are you Ashmi Evans?"

The sweetest smile broke across Alex's face. I was mesmerized. "Yes. It's nice to put a face to the voice over the phone. Please call me Ash and she, her." As Alex stood, I took in their height and lean, muscular physique and had to wonder at the attraction I was feeling. These were not the attributes that usually drew me to someone, yet here I was, surprising feels in my belly and below.

Alex extended a hand out to me and so I shook it. Their grasp was firm as they spoke. "It's a pleasure to meet you, welcome to Desjardins' Garden. Sounded like you have quite the plan for The Frisky Bean."

I did have quite the plan for the café a few doors down. That was what I was known for, after all. "It's what I do. As I explained on the phone, I consider myself an influencer of influencers on social media. I create pop-up experiences all over Los Angeles and have even begun expanding to other cities as well. Social media influencers vie to get an invite to one of my events, and businesses want to be chosen for all of the free promotions. As soon as I discovered it, I knew The Frisky Bean was the perfect location for one of my events. Do you go there often since you are located so close?"

They gave me a lopsided smile. "Too often. It's probably not very good for me, but I can't resist all of the yummy goodness and can't function without my midday jolt of caffeine." They winked.

Such a good-natured cutie. Adorable. "It's good that you are versed in what they serve. With their risqué food options and décor, the theme I am going for is a lush, sensual garden experience."

"I thought that might be a possibility and worked up some different designs, three of which lean in that direction. Sit there and I'll be right back with the designs." They pointed to a small, round, distressed white-washed table with a couple of matching chairs set off to the side.

I took a seat, but something about the abrupt order rubbed me the wrong way. Actually, I knew why that was the case. I was having inappropriate desirous feelings toward Alex and I was used to giving commands, not taking them from my partners. So, despite my initial reaction, I was going to likely have to put those thoughts away and focus solely on our working relationship. It was doubtful that someone like Alex would be interested in submitting to me. A pity, that. But, refocus I did.

2

BUSINESS FIRST

Alex

I WAS FINDING it hard to stay focused on the job. Ash was a stunner. She had a light, warm brown skin tone and deep brown eyes rimmed with full dark-brown lashes. The blunt, thick dark-brown bangs framed them perfectly so there was no missing the bold, direct look of confidence. Most intriguing. I'd already been mildly infatuated by a voice over the phone, but now I felt utterly enthralled.

"Here are the three ideas I had for your event." I handed her the sketches I'd drawn. One was inspired by the rainforest. An oasis of lush orchids and other wildflowers, big leaf greenery, and a special water feature I could assemble created a warm escape into fantasy and adventure. The second was inspired by a secret garden. Roses, ivy, woven vines, and lavender all played into hidden spaces, vertical features, and surprising treasures. The last was inspired by my heritage—the bright colors of the Bruges tulip market. Years ago, my extended family, who still lives in Bruges, provided a friend of mine with bulbs for their tulip farm in Washington state. Part of the deal ensured I would have discounted prices on acquiring the beautiful and unique tulips. The proposal showed that the arrangements would be set up throughout the café to give the air of visiting one of these fields for a sexy picnic amongst the blooms. The riotous colors gave it a time-out-of-life feel.

After explaining them all, I sat back and let Ash study and consider the options while I covertly studied and considered her. It had been a while since I'd had such a visceral attraction to someone. The way she contemplated each proposal so intensely had me wanting her to turn that same intensity onto me. *Study me. Choose me.*

My internal monologue deserved a severe eye roll, so I shook my head to clear all those unprofessional and probably irrelevant thoughts. The likelihood that she would be equally attracted to me and into the things I needed was so slim. And, I shouldn't have these thoughts about a client in the first place.

Eventually, she looked up, and I was thankful that she appeared pleased. Resolute. "I'd like the tulips," she said with a certainty that made my insides clench. "The other two designs are tempting and beautiful, but also the more predictable routes. The tulips are unexpected, and I love to give people the unexpected. If anyone found my events predictable, that would be the end of my job. On top of that, I love the way you have used the flowers to create pockets of intimacy and whimsy. Plus... the food at the café will be perfect for a casual picnic leading to some smexy times amongst the tulips."

I would jump for joy, but that would be highly inappropriate. Okay. Not as inappropriate as what I'd been thinking about, but still a very unprofessional look, so instead I said, "I'm so glad you chose that one. I agree it will be something more unique and having studied some of your earlier events, I thought you might be up for it."

Her smile was tender, but her lifted eyebrow was... arrogant? "You looked into me after we talked? Why?"

Why—exactly! Why did I feel like there was a right and a wrong answer to this? Or maybe, all the answers were wrong and I'd be in trouble for any of them? I internally shook these thoughts off as well and replied, "I like to be prepared. I always try to get to know more about my clients before I work on my proposals. It can give me an edge if they are shopping around for the right florist to meet their needs. I'm sure you do your research before choosing a location to host a pop-up or inviting an influencer to one of your events."

Her eyes gleamed with mirth, but that eyebrow still demanded answers. "Touché. Are you sure you will have all of these colorful tulips before the event?"

"Yes. They will be shipped directly from my friend up north and should arrive with plenty of time for them to look healthy and vibrant." I tried to cover up how much her intense focus on me, now that I had it, affected me. I wanted to defer. To drop down to my knees and place my head into her lap and my well-being into her seemingly capable hands for a time. I wanted to give her whatever she needed or wanted from me.

I wanted those things not to scare her away. Not as a client but also not as... more. I couldn't risk the more, so I stuck with the client. "If you want some referrals for past clientele with around the same budget events, I am happy to provide those to you. I want you to feel confident with the quality you can expect working with Desjardins' Garden."

The twinkle was still in her eyes, but a smirk joined in. "How many people call you on your store name meaning garden's garden?"

I smirked back. "Not very many. It's like a community secret for those of us who know. I mostly amused myself when creating it."

"I would like to be notified the instant you get the flowers in so that I might inspect them myself. You will find me a very hands-on client. I prefer to control the process so that I can control the outcome. Will that be a problem?" That arrogant brow went up again and my insides twisted.

"That shouldn't be a problem at all. As soon as they arrive, I'll call you so that you can come." I hadn't meant to make that sound as dirty as it did. When I realized what I'd said, I was sure my cheeks had to be turning pink.

"You can be sure, I always come."

The grin she gave me was pure sin. Or, was I reading what I wanted into it? Stay focused. The business. This was a big client. Great growth opportunities. I was definitely experiencing some growth opportunities. Gah. Why was it so hard? No! Not hard. Stop it. It was so challenging to stay focused.

Deep breath in. And out. "I look forward to working with you. Please sign the proposal you liked, and I'll send you some more specific plans for each section of the café for you to approve."

She signed and was out the door too fast. I didn't get to say anything more to her as someone new had entered to buy a birthday bouquet for their loved one.

I should be elated about the new contract, and a part of me was, but alongside that, I felt a bit sad that I hadn't had a chance to say goodbye. *But, it wasn't goodbye, was it?* That perked me right back up.

3

WELL... HELLO

Ash

I FINALLY GOT THE CALL. *The* call! It felt like I'd been waiting forever for them to call me and a few days before my event, I heard from Alex. You'd think I hadn't been busy in the weeks leading up to this event with the way thoughts of them kept popping into my head.

In truth, I'd been working closely with Summer and Kevin, the co-owners of The Frisky Bean, to set up a specific catering menu for the event. It will include some new items created in honor of my culture from my mother's side of the family. Dishes like Cheeky Chikki, a peanut brittle dessert that will be formed into little butts. The Jale-be-mine is where Kevin will make traditional jalebi but into a spiral heart and then dipped into a syrup infused with rose so they will come out red. I couldn't wait to see all of what they would do with what we talked about.

I'd also been sending out invitations to the various influencers I thought would be perfect for this event. I'd gotten a few extra spon-sors involved. All-in-all, I had kept super busy. And yet. And yet, in the background of all that work, one gentle, flower-loving person intruded regularly into my thoughts.

However, none of those thoughts had prepared me for my first sight of Alex today, nor for the instant lust that gripped me. Alex was wearing a strapless summer dress. It had a fitted top with a floaty, knee-length skirt in a soft blue that matched their eyes. Their hair was less floppy and more artfully arranged curls, and there was a smattering of pink blush and brown liner illustrating their gorgeous face. The glossy nude lips that smiled nervously at me were so damn kissable. Every instinct made me want to see their softness in a different setting and all for me.

Focus! Say something before this gets awkward. It is already awkward. Gah. "You look beautiful, like one of your flowers." *What did you just say? Are we writing sonnets next?* Too thrown off to notice until I replayed the scene in my mind later, I missed the way Alex glowed under my praise. I was too busy berating myself for turning a working relationship weird. *Remember why you're here.* "Show me the tulips." *Well, that was rude. Wasn't it?*

I didn't miss how Alex scurried to comply with what was essentially a command. I didn't miss how they looked to me for approval when indicating the tulips. They were taking my breath away. With one step into the cold workroom, I was met with a cacophony of brilliant colors from reds to purples and everything in between. They were vibrant and joyful and perky--and so were the blooms. I didn't miss one damn thing.

I stepped farther in so I could focus more fully on the blooms. Breathtaking. I turned to Alex to praise the flowers and found I was staring at their shoulder. They had come up behind me closer than I'd realized. I had to turn my head up so I could look into their perfectly lined puppy-dog eyes. I tried. I really tried not to go there. I totally went there. "You did such a good job," I purred.

Their eyes went round and their joyful smile was almost blinding.

I had to keep going, had to. "Do you like me praising you, Alex?"

They took a moment to think about it, never losing eye contact with me. Then, they looked down bashfully and nodded. They were so tall and muscular and, apparently, desirous of my praise. I wanted to give it to them and see them melt for me, my praise, my commands. I found I wanted them to be mine. To get to know them intimately, emotionally, and mentally in the ways that worked for us both.

"May I command you, Alex? Give you direction? Reward and punish you as I see fit within your boundaries? Nothing extreme for now as we are still new to one another." I waited to see if I had pushed too far. I hadn't realized exactly how tense I had been, holding completely still for their answer, until they responded and I was able to relax again.

"I would like that. My safe word is daffodil."

A snort laugh escaped me. "Of course it is. When do you get off work today, Alex?"

"The store closes at six-thirty. I have some work to do in the back until seven-thirty. That's when I usually grab some dinner and head home." They looked up again and the hope there made me want to close the shop right then to explore this, but it would be better and more respectful to wait.

"I'll come by right before closing time. Does that work for you?"

Their enthusiastic, "Yes!" came through loud and clear. "But... what about the work I need to do in the back?"

"Oh. Don't worry. I'll make sure you still get it done." I was looking forward to it, but they didn't need to know that.

"In that case, my yes still stands." They blushed and I loved my effect on them.

"I would like to reward you. May I touch your face?"

"Yes!" Another wildly enthusiastic response. They were so sweet, my heart hurt.

I reached out to caress their cheek and was gifted by the way their face instantly leaned into my caress, eyes closed. Like the moment was too precious to do anything but record it to memory. *Same, sweet one. Same.*

"I will see you tonight, then."

They looked so sad as they responded, "Yes, I suppose so."

I walked away without looking back, lest their big, needy eyes pull me right back in to give them what they silently begged for. That was what I enjoyed about this dynamic, after all: providing what my partners needed, being the one in charge of giving them everything.

Alex was so much more than I had bargained for when we first met. Tonight couldn't come fast enough. What else was I going to learn about them?

4

____

SURRENDER

Alex

FOR THE REST of the day, I replayed the gentle caress Ash had given me, the power of her... well... just her as she waited for my response, the calm confidence that emanated from her every pore. This was a person I could sink into for a time and know that she would take good care of me.

There might have been a few headshakes throughout the day attempting to clear all of those thoughts from my head so I could concentrate on my work. But the anticipation was evergreen.

I had to wonder how many of my customers were accidentally on the receiving end of one of my besotted, near-distant looks.

Oh well. It was too late to worry about all that. The clock was counting down as slow as molasses and I was on the move toward the front door of the shop to lock it and set the sign to closed. I could feel the disappointment trying to ivy its way in, but I held firm that she was a good person and if she wasn't there, it was because of something important.

I was about to turn the key when I yelped, a little, nothing overly dramatic. It was startling, as I looked through the glass door, to find a pair of intense brown eyes looking back at me. No. Looking seems too weak a word. More like... smoldering. Eating me up. A shiver of excitement climbed the full length of my spine, culminating in one of my lopsided smiles.

She came.

My heart was in full "Oh my god! It's happening! Everybody remain calm!" mode from *The Office*.

I locked up behind her, turning the sign to closed. Twirling around, I found her closer to me than I had anticipated. We studied each other, speaking volumes with just our eyes. Warmth permeated everywhere, as though she were touching me in all those spots. My instincts were all over the place. A part of me wanted to drop to my knees and give myself over to her already. Another part warned that we weren't there yet, that she was still also a client and that any transition from client to something else would need some verbal communication and agreement.

Torn, I did what I had earlier in the day and submitted a little by dropping my gaze to the ground and waiting for her to let me know what she was thinking, wanting, or needing. There was a second advantage to this, which was that I could study what she was wearing. She'd been quite casual earlier in the day, but she came back wearing a pair of dark-gray slacks and a white button-down shirt cuffed at the sleeves and unbuttoned to the center of her chest. She had on a multi-string silver necklace where each strand progressively got longer, culminating in one that dangled a string of metal into her shirt. How far down did it extend? Her navel? Past it? Did it attach to anything lower? I was mesmerized by that detail alone. Well, I would have been if she wasn't also wearing dark-gray suspenders over her shirt. Suspenders! Why was that so hot?

Lastly, I was able to study her shoes. In continuation of her feminine twist on masculine clothing, she was wearing bright-red stilettos. It was a toss-up as to which affected me more: the fact that I found them exceedingly sexy on her or the fact that I was jealous I wasn't wearing them because I was sure they'd look sexy on me too. I would definitely be investing in a pair in the near future.

She finally broke our silent exchange. "Do I have permission to touch you? Your face again? Your arms? Are you still okay with me taking charge, Alexandre?"

Hearing my full name on her lips melted all of my insides into puddles of liquid hearts. I nodded and said, "Yes. Please."

"Good. Then... first things first. Let's get comfortable." Ashmi led me by the hand to the back where my office was located. Once there, she proceeded to my couch, sat, and pointed at the floor near her feet. She didn't need to ask me twice.

I knelt and it felt like stunning relief to finally be where I'd wanted to be for weeks. She pointed at her lap, so I laid my head down on her thigh and breathed a sigh full of pleasure and contentment. Underlying those feelings and staying dormant, but not for long, was an intense desire.

Ash began running her fingers through my curls as she carefully negotiated with me. We discussed things in such detail, and her fingers were so soothing, that I lost track of time completely.

When we were finished, she ran her hand through one more time before yanking my head back with a firm grip. I was staring into her beautiful, compelling eyes just inches away. I was utterly speechless.

"You have been such a good darling, sitting at my feet all evening. Come. I want to reward you. Straddle me."

I did. And I waited.

"Such a precious darling."

I loved that she called me that. I was totally smitten and wanted to stay her darling. Was it too early to add the word "always" to the end of that thought? Maybe so, but it was what I was feeling nonetheless.

5

———————————

ATTACHMENT

Ash

I'D HAD plenty of subs before, but something about Alex's submission was affecting me in ways that were utterly unexpected and wholly right. They seemed to have everything I always looked for and rarely found in one person. I was as impatient to know them today as I might a month from now.

I pulled their head down toward mine and commanded, "Kiss me. Deeply. Passionately."

And they did. Alex followed my demand to perfection. As gentle as they'd been until then, they were fierce in their thorough tasting of my mouth. It was so wonderful, I almost lost myself in the kiss. Almost. But a girl likes what she likes and I liked being in control. I grabbed Alex's hair at the scalp and yanked them an inch back so we were no longer touching. "Good darling."

Joy was obvious on their expressive face as I praised them. We had negotiated wanting to have sex and I was still working out exactly what, when, and how that would happen. Alex's cock was hard and lying on my belly. I reached under the skirt of their dress, caressing their leg every inch of the way. They held utterly still, but their whole body vibrated with the effort they were exerting to do so.

"Are you still comfortable with what we are doing?"

"Yes, Ash. I am more than comfortable. Eager."

"That makes me happy to hear, darling. I prefer you eager. Always." I gently caressed along the side of their penis, feeling it jerk. "You feel so soft. Like silk." I pulled their head down so I could whisper in their ear, "Turns out my good darling has a naughty side. Have you been wearing a dress commando all day?"

"Yes, Ash." The slightest tremor of angst at their admission quivered under my fingertips. "I enjoy the feel and freedom of being bare. In a dress, no one knows but me."

"And now me."

"Yes."

"I want to take you and make you feel so good now. Get off my lap and sit where I am." I let go and, per Alex's charm, they followed my direction exactly. After divesting myself of my pants and underwear, I grabbed a condom from my pocket and straddled Alex. Their dress was bunched around their waist so I was able to roll the condom onto their penis. "I've been thinking about you since I left earlier. I've been wet for hours, darling."

I grabbed onto their hair again and tilted their chin up so we were watching each other as I sank down, enveloping their cock. Without much foreplay, the stretch burned a little, but I hadn't been lying about being wet for my sweet darling for so long that I couldn't wait any longer. "You are mine tonight, Alexandre."

"Yes, Ash. For longer if you'll have me."

"I..." I rolled my hips carefully, prolonging our pleasure. "...would like that too."

I caressed, praised, and held my darling Alex while simultaneously riding and playing with my clit until we both came apart in powerful, rolling waves. Cradled in my arms, they sighed with such contentment, that I felt its echo in my chest.

It felt like a signal, a social media post that reads, "Tonight, I started something new. Wish me luck," rolled up with the reply, "I wish I could like this ten thousand more times."

6

BEGINNING

Alex

IT WAS a couple of days later and I was still replaying every minute of my interaction with Ash. Good thing I was a good multitasker since I was busy bringing my creation to life in The Frisky Bean. Summer and Kevin, the co-owners of the café, welcomed me and had been nothing but supportive as I transformed their space. As indicated in the design, using the brightly colored tulips mixed with the tables, I was able to create little pockets for "picnics."

I'd seen when Ash had arrived. Of course. I was so very attuned to her presence already. She crossed the room, her confidence radiating out of her every step. There could be no doubt in anyone's mind who was running this show.

"Hello, Alex. It is a pleasure... seeing your vision come to life."

There was no doubt in my head that her small pause was purposeful. "I was just working with your instruction, Ash." I'm pretty sure my eyes were filled with hearts for those who knew how to see them.

"You do a good job of it."

"I try."

What was happening? Apparently, we were going to openly flirt using event dialogue as our flimsy-ass cover. I could tell as soon as playtime was over and she reverted into her no-nonsense, social media influencer of influencers.

"I'd like you to fill out tables five and six. They're in prime spots and I want them to overflow with tulips. We have about fifteen minutes before people will begin to show. Can you do that for me?" It was all business until that last line, and then her voice was all smooth velvet, like a rose petal. I just wanted to roll around in that voice.

"I can do that. Anything else you need? Anything at all?"

"Meet me after the event to celebrate our success?"

"I wouldn't miss it, Ash."

"Good. Now be a—darling, and take care of those tables." I heard that pause loud and clear once again. Ash was so freaking—gah—wonderful.

Shortly thereafter, a couple of vendors that were also invited to the event showed up and arranged their displays. I made sure to provide a tulip background for them as well. Soon, those influencers that were invited arrived. They mingled, filmed, pictured, ate, networked, and raved over yet another spectacular event.

Everyone loved the food from The Frisky Bean, and there was nothing but good things to say about the customer service. Considering Summer's bubbly, friendly personality, I wasn't surprised.

I spent much of my time people-watching from the corner of the café. I especially enjoyed seeing Ashmi doing her thing. She ruled so casually. It was part and parcel of who she was. Everyone flocked to her strength of will, but I couldn't help but smile, knowing it was all for me later. Thrilling.

Kevin sidled up to me, having finished in the kitchen much earlier. He was the head baker and also a good friend. "Honey. You got it bad for Miss Thing over there, huh?"

"Maybe."

He rolled his eyes, but it was good-natured ribbing.

"I may or may not be meeting her after this event."

"Now, that's what I'm talking about. I told Summer the other day we should try to set you two up, but it looks like you beat us to it."

Kevin was such a beautiful man inside and out. If either of us enjoyed topping, we probably would have tried dating each other when we first met. But, it was pretty clear that we weren't compatible that way so we became friends instead.

Now, Ashmi, we were perfectly compatible. My phone buzzed, so I pulled it out, and it was a text from Ash. I read it and flushed head to toe with excitement.

ASHMI

You should strap in later for what I have planned. Oh, wait. No. I'll be the one strapping in.

I MAY HAVE FORGOTTEN that Kevin was even there, but he got the gist of the text from my reaction and patted me on the shoulder. "Good for you. Have fun, kids." He strode off with those parting words, but I thought I heard wistfulness in his tone. I would have to ask him about that sometime. For now, I sought out Ash, and when our gazes met, I flushed all over again and looked away with a grin.

ASH

The amount of buzz this event generated on social media was beyond even my expectations. People couldn't stop talking about the florals, wanting to taste the food, commenting "for free" in regard to the sensual shots highlighting the sexy food names, and more. Posts left and right were going viral, and the hashtag "#thefriskybeanpicnic" was trending. I was damn proud of all of us who worked to make this happen.

But, when I looked over at Alex across the room, curls flopping once again and sparkly gems glued to the corner of their eyes, shining like the gem they were, the thing I was most excited by at that moment was the flush and smile I'd inspired with one text and one look.

My favorite arrangement out of this was us.

FRISKY ENGAGEMENT

1

PLANS

Lisa

"YOU MEAN SO MUCH to me. I'm not sure how my day could go on without you. The way you bring joy into my life is—"

"Are you going to keep making verbal love to it, or are you going to eat one of our latest delicacies?"

"Both? 'Both' is good, I hear." I returned with a saucy wink. "Right. So where were we my oh-so-tasty hamantaschen? What are you calling this again?"

"Kiss My Haman-tuchus." Summer Palmer, the co-owner of my favorite coffee shop and bakery, The Frisky Bean, answered looking rather amused. Her red hair was half up with little escaped curls framing her face. I'd been too distracted by the adorable, curve-hugging dress with a sheer layer of blue over a floral pattern she wore when I first walked in to even notice her hair, though.

"Do you think Jason would approve of me kissing your Haman-tuchus?" I threw in an air kiss to underscore my words.

If I wasn't already practically engaged, if she wasn't also in a serious relationship, *and* if she wasn't straight, then I'd be tempted. Of course, the woman I intended to ask to marry me would have probably welcomed the threesome since we had very similar tastes in partners and Summer's joyful personality would have fit right in.

It didn't hurt to harmlessly flirt though. Camila would find the retelling of it amusing.

Summer giggled and leaned in conspiratorially, "Lisa! You know he is a bit too territorial for that, but don't worry, my tuchus gets plenty of kisses."

"If you say so. I guess I'll have to settle for this pointy treat instead. Please explain the amazing flavors going on in this thing."

Summer perked up too fast, hitting her hand on the counter and yelping, before answering, "This one is made with a sweet cinnamon-orange marmalade inside of a traditional triangular crust and topped with a dark chocolate kiss that melts into it as it bakes."

"Melt my heart." I bit into the treat and the rich flavors were divine.

Leaning across the counter again, Summer whispered, "Tell me again, what you had in mind. I'm so excited for you!" She practically squealed the last part at me. Her enthusiasm was adorable, but nothing could beat my joy and anticipation.

I finished off my last bite, and there may have been a moan in there, too, before I responded, "I would like to propose to Camila at your Purim party. I plan to surprise her with a flower crown from Desjardin's Garden next door. I've already talked to Alex, and what they designed is so freaking beautiful. You'll absolutely love it. Oh! Also, Alex said they have some ideas on how to add a few subtle floral accents for ambiance and that it was their gift to the event."

"That's so nice of them! I was wondering how I wanted to decorate. I'll talk to Alex and make sure we get the place in a style befitting the holiday and the proposal. Are you presenting her with a ring? God, I love love." She put both hands in front of her and made a heart symbol.

"Yes. I have the perfect ring ordered for her. She's going to be so happy. She once showed me a picture of her great-grandparents. Despite only knowing them briefly, they left quite an impression on my love and she adores telling their stories. I zoomed in on the image of her great-grandmother's hand to recreate a similar ring."

Summer imitated melting behind the counter. "You've made me all gooey with how sweet that is. I'm going to mush to the ground now."

I couldn't help but to chuckle at her antics until she leaned a bit too far and fell into the case.

I winced.

She winced.

She quickly straightened up and said, "Why don't you shoot me an email with all of your ideas and we can hash it out over the next few days."

I was just saying, "Sounds good," when the door opened and I was so happy we were done talking about all my grand plans because the most beautiful woman in the world walked in. At the very least, she was the most beautiful in mine. Standing only five foot one with brown, wavy short hair, brown joyful eyes, and lips I always craved to kiss, Camila Ximena Garcia Ramirez always took my breath away. Especially when she came from the first morning yoga session she taught. Dressed in leggings and a sports bra, she usually had a casual elegance to her, which I also loved, but she glowed so much after yoga.

"Camila! Get over here, sweetie. You have to try this new treat!" I was pretty sure I'd saved the moment and she didn't suspect a thing. She raced over and kissed me before turning her attention to the tray of treats. I wasn't sure how I was going to contain my excitement all week long because I truly sucked at having secrets, but I reminded myself that it would be worth it. I couldn't wait to see her face when I asked and when she saw her ring.

Gah! It's so hard not spilling the beans! Maybe I should ask her right now. No. You have to do this right. Camila deserves all the romance in the world. Right. So... No spilling the beans. Maybe I should keep a bit busier than usual so I have less opportunities to mess this up.

I looked over to find Camila and Summer looking directly at me like they were waiting for me to speak. "Did I miss a question?" Summer looked highly amused. Camila looked pretty amused herself, if I'm being honest. "What did I miss?"

2

PLANS TAKE TWO

Camila

WHAT WAS UP WITH LISA? She might look killer with her blonde bob clipped back on one side with a teal gem comb, her blue eyes lined in subtle brown natural makeup, and her lightly tanned cheeks barely highlighted with a pink blush. Her tall, full-figured body was stunning in a low-cut, body-hugging teal dress with a lower thigh peplum. She was always the epitome of fashion which suited her job as a personal stylist. I don't think I've ever seen her outside the house looking less than immaculate. We were quite the pair, but I wouldn't change a thing. Of course, I wouldn't try to count all of our shoes, either. Between her heels, my flats, and our mutual obsession with having footwear options, it would take a long, long while.

Today she was wearing a strappy white pump that matched the pearls circling her neck with a string of more pearls trailing between her breasts disappearing inside of her dress. If we were alone I would worship every inch of that trail with my tongue. My stomach clenched at the thought. This woman was my bashert, my soulmate, my other half. She was also the vixen that took possession of me so completely in the bedroom and I loved her for it.

Seeing her distracted was just plain weird. She was usually the most observant person I knew, so it felt bizarre for her to be lost in any conversation. *What has her so distracted?* "Earth to Lisa Hannah Berg. What were you thinking about?"

I could swear she had to think about it before answering, but she finally said, "Still distracted by how absolutely tasty the Kiss My Haman-Tuchus is. You really must try it."

Okay. Now I knew her mind was somewhere else. "Babe. I did try it. Let's replay the last few minutes." I stuck another bite in my mouth, moaned and said, "Wow. Summer. This is divine. Hey, babe. What did you think?" I gave her a pointed look. "And, that's where we left off. Is everything okay? It's not like you to—"

"Right. Sorry. I have been dealing with a very finicky client and all morning my brain has been half-working on what and whom to dress her in for her next interview. She's quite nervous about it." Lisa fidgeted with one of her bracelets and I knew she wasn't telling me the real reason. After a beat, though, my confidant goddess was back. "As far as the new Purim treat, I thought it was delicious. A gift from the big G." She winked playfully and I couldn't help but smile back.

"Just like you babe." I winked back.

"The delicious or the gift part?" She stepped closer and the air between us crackled with energy.

"Yes." This woman gave me life. She *really* did.

From the side, there came a throat clearing. I looked over to find Summer, cheeks pink, eyes wide, smiling at our antics. "I'd give you my office, but that is a Jason and Summer space only. Sorry."

Before I could get a word out, Lisa swiftly said, "I have to run anyway." She pulled me in for a hug and a quick kiss on the lips. I was convinced she was about to sprint out the door. Instead, she paused long enough to tilt my face up with the crook of her finger and said, "I plan to have us be very bad later so be good for me while I'm gone."

My panties melted away and I stammered back, "I'll be the best."

She gave me another, firmer kiss and walked out of The Frisky Bean.

I slowly turned to Summer, "What just happened?"

Fanning herself, she responded, "One of my romance novels came to life in front of me?"

I snorted. "Does this mean we're the main characters and you're comic rel—"

Summer mock glared. "If you finish that sentence, no coffee for you."

I mimicked zippering my lips, but underneath we were both containing our mirth. "I don't know that I've ever seen Lisa so distracted, though. Do you know what that was really about?"

Suspiciously, Summer got very busy tiding. "Nope."

"Uh. Huh." Clearly, I wasn't going to learn anything from her. I needed to move on to a new topic anyway before I had to head back for the next class I was in charge of. Now that Lisa wasn't here, I could have the private conversation I'd meant to have with Summer for a few days. "Hey. So... I have a favor to ask of you."

"Shoot. I'm happy to help."

Now I fidgeted a bit with one of the curls at the nape of my neck. A habit since childhood I'd mostly stopped doing, but it still showed up when I was stressed or nervous. Check to both of those. "I was hoping that it would be okay with you if I asked Lisa to marry me at your Purim party."

Summer suddenly choked on, well, nothing. She hadn't eaten or drunk anything, but there she was spluttering.

Her voice came out a bit higher-pitched when she said, "Um. Yes. Of course. That sounds great. What... ummm... what were you wanting to plan? Is this your first Purim since converting?"

"It's actually my second since then, but I've been attending them for many years due to my friend's family hosting these super fun celebrations with costumes that, as a kid in Mexico, I had to be a part of. Which is why, I was thinking that maybe you could have a costume contest, it being Purim and all, and while we are in front of everyone, I can pop the question. What do you think?"

In hindsight, I probably should have realized there was something up with the way Summer responded, but at the time, I was so excited and nervous for what I was planning, her smirk didn't register. Neither did the interesting way she responded. "I'll take care of everything. Make sure you have coordinating costumes."

"Okay. I can do that. I was thinking we could come as Mercedes de Acosta and Greta Garbo." Just imagining Lisa dressed as a 1930s starlet made my mouth water. One hunger I *could* appease, so I popped the last bite into my mouth.

Summer let out a squeal of sorts. "Those are the perfect costumes! This will be so much fun!" If there was an extra twinkle in her eyes, I wouldn't have noticed because I checked my watch and realized I was going to be late if I didn't hurry. "Oh! I have to run. Thanks, Summer! You're the best."

"I can't wait to see you both at the party. Write me and let me know what you need from me."

"Will do."

Laughter from behind me as I walked out couldn't permeate my concentration figuring out all the things I would need to get in place for us to have a proposal we'd both remember.

3

____

SWEET SURPRISE

Lisa

"PLEASE TELL me we are still on schedule for the ring." I might have sounded mildly desperate on the phone call. I tried to cover it, but no one likes to hear their carefully laid plans were experiencing some potential delays.

"We should still be okay with the previously scheduled delivery, though it will be tight," Tabitha responded.

Tabitha Chase and I had worked together for a while regarding dressing some of my clients. I liked the unique fashion the company she worked for provided. One of the things they were known for was creating custom pieces of clothes or jewelry. Since we were becoming friends as well, I had turned to her and her staff to help me create the ring for Camila. Unfortunately, the fine detail engraver I wanted to use for her immaculate skills had a family situation she had to attend to. "Okay. Thank you for the update. I hope whatever she is dealing with, will get resolved quickly."

"I'm sure it will. Have I mentioned how excited I am to be a part of your engagement?"

"No. I didn't know you were coming to the party."

"Oh, absolutely. Sean and I wouldn't miss it. We love a Purim celebration. When we were growing up, we used to fight over who would have the best costume, who could win the most carnival games, and we once even fought over who could eat the most hamantaschen. Man. We were a menace to each other."

"I love how you say that in the past tense. From everything I've seen and heard, you two still like to go at each other—wait, that sounded wrong. What I meant to say is that you two still enjoy pounding each other—nope, still not right. I meant that you two both like to end up on top—you know what, I give up. You get my drift." Tabitha wasn't given to wild displays of levity, but she had laughed a bit at my innuendos so that was a major accomplishment.

"We definitely know how to tackle any challenge and derive a great amount of satisfaction from finishing each other."

"Touché."

"Don't worry about the ring. I'll stay on top of it and let you know if anything else comes up."

A part of me wanted to respond in a panic. *What did she mean if anything else comes up? Is there something else that might come up? What did she know?* Another, more rational, part of me took over before I did that and I was able to calmly say, "Great. Thank you. I'll talk to you soon."

With only a week until the party, there were a lot of little details to take care of, and I wanted everything to be perfect.

A couple hours later, I had managed the details and even signed a contract with a new client, when Camila strolled into my home office holding some garment bags.

"Guess what I picked up while I was out?" She looked giddy and flushed and oh so beautiful.

"From the garment bags, I can only conclude a new couch?"

Her nose crinkled as she made the most adorable face. "Har, har. I got our costumes for the party."

"I hadn't realized we had decided on costumes yet." It was odd that Camila would choose something to do with style, especially for both of us, without discussing it first. I didn't want to rain on her parade, though, since she was so clearly happy about it.

"I know. I know. But, I knew these would be perfect and I wanted to surprise you."

She stood there with no indication that she was planning to open the bags so I joked, "Aaand? Aren't you going to show me what you got?"

"Nope! You are going to have to trust me and let me surprise you that day." She gave me the most saucy look and walked out heading toward our bedroom.

What the hell? "You get your pretty ass back here!" I was out of my seat.

"Nope! Come and get me."

My panties grew moist. I loved her bratty side as much as I loved her sweet side. "You can keep your secret, but when I get to the bedroom, I'll expect you on your knees to make up for tempting my curiosity and leaving me completely unsatisfied." I headed the other direction stopping in the kitchen to grab a cup full of ice. If she was in the mood to play, so was I. "I'm coming."

"Not yet you're not."

"You are so saucy today. I'm sure I can find alternative uses for such a playful tongue." I enjoyed getting into topspace. I was a bit of a control personality type, but life could often feel so out of control. Here, with Camila, I could feel like everything would always be okay. She gave me that and it made everything else manageable.

"I am ready and happy to please you, mistress."

And there she was, a sight on her knees, completely naked and mine. Her skin still had a glow about it from her running around. Her curls were tousled by the wind and my hand itched to run through them. I walked over and placed the cup down on the nightstand.

"Reach under my skirt and pull down my panties, love." Her hands were a bit cold on my heated flesh as she began to do as I commanded. She stroked the outside of my thighs on her way back down and my lower belly clenched at her touch. "Good girl."

She looked at me with mischief in her eyes and tossed the underwear basketball-style into the hamper. "Score."

"Not if you keep doing things like that you won't."

"Right. Sorry mistress."

It had taken us some time to develop the relationship that worked best for us, but we both enjoyed this dynamic. She was playful and not always the best submissive which gave me opportunities to be a bit bitchy or stern. She was never extremely bratty and that was good because I wasn't interested in being a brat tamer. This subtle pull and tug between us had been refined over our years together. Comfortable but never boring. My heart was getting as heated as my pussy thinking about it.

I leaned against our mattress and inched my skirt up. Her eyes couldn't stay downcast. She tried at first, but the higher my skirt went, the more she simply stared in open lust. She could wait a little longer. Bared to her, I began playing with my folds. Spreading them and massaging my clit gently. As her eyes devoured me, I opened my legs further to give her something to feast on. "Do you want to join in, love?"

Her voice was no longer playful but husky as she answered, "Yes. Please."

It was tempting to let her do so, but I had brought the ice for a good reason. I stopped and pushed my skirt back down. Her disappointment was palatable. "You'll get your wish in just a minute. First, lean over the bed with your arms behind your back and your legs wide."

She got into position so swiftly, that I had to work to stop myself from laughing at her eagerness. From inside our nightstand drawer, I pulled out a condom and ripped it open. She was probably a bit confused or thought we were about to use a dildo or something, but that was not my plan. This was a gentle punishment after all. I like when my plans come together and this one was going to be oh-so sweet.

4

———————————

HOT AND COLD

Camila

I WASN'T sure what to expect, but when I'd gotten home with our costumes, I could tell that Lisa was on edge so I purposefully instigated this playtime. Honestly, I could use it too. I wasn't usually one to take on too many planning things and all the myriad details to be in charge of, so trying to plan the perfect engagement was taking a toll and I needed to clear my head. Feel free for a bit.

That didn't mean I always knew what the outcome of my playfulness would be and this was one of those times. It's not like I hadn't seen the ice cubes she'd brought in with her, I had, but there were so many fun ways to use them on each other, that I couldn't have guessed what she planned next. Like... why did she need a condom? Was the ice for later? Was she getting a dildo? I took a deep breath and remembered, I wasn't responsible for figuring it out, I could trust in her and let go. So, I did.

I was sinking into my submission when one of her hands landed on my back holding my arms in place and the other, "Oh shit! That's so cold!"

"Isn't it though?" She sounded quite satisfied with herself.

I had to take some deep breaths as my body tried to adjust to having ice cubes inside of my very hot pussy. As far as I could tell, she'd placed a few in a condom and the sensation of hot and cold felt like burning but also, holy hell, it felt so damn good. My pussy was clenching around them trying to figure out what to do. I only had a short time to contemplate it, though, before she pulled me back off the bed and with her hand in my curls, directed me back to my knees.

She was in front of me with her skirt back up and her legs wide a moment later. "Keep those inside of you while you put your hot mouth to pleasuring me. Just your mouth for now. I'll tell you when you can move your arms from behind your back. Let me know if it becomes unbearable."

I was able to squeak out, "I will." I was hers so completely. I was in pain, I was in pleasure, and now I was allowed to give her pleasure. Everything was on overload so my brain shut down, and I did exactly as she asked of me. I loved the taste of her, the smell of her, and hearing her moan as I sucked a little harder on her clit. I, in turn, groaned each time I clenched around the cold torment inside of me. I lost track of time and simply felt the moment in every way.

"Release your hands and fuck me."

I plunged two and then three fingers into her wet pussy as I continued to lick and suck on her clit.

"Fist me."

I added a fourth finger and as she stretched to accommodate me, growing even wetter, I aligned my fingers and was able to get my small, fine-boned hand in without needing lube this time. I wrapped my other arm around her big thigh and held her as close as possible so she wouldn't buck away. I aimed for her g-spot with yoga-pose precision and a few pumps of my fist along with a grazing of my teeth on her clit later, she shattered and the spasms gripped my hand. I slipped out as she came down.

She was completely pink on her chest and neck above her dress. I'd done that. She was still catching her breath when she turned around and ordered me to undo the back of her dress. As the dress fell away, she was beautifully nude with just a lacy bra. Her soft stomach was before my face and I couldn't stop myself from placing a kiss on her belly button.

"Did I say you could kiss me?"

"No. My kiss went astray, I suppose."

Her snort brought a smile to my own face. "How's the ice darling?"

"I think you made me so hot for you that it melted completely."

"Good. Now climb on the bed, hands above your head, and legs wide." She took a minute to pull out the condom and remove her bra. As she climbed onto the bed, her full breasts bounced and I wanted to get my mouth on them but didn't move. She'd been quite clear about what she wanted me to do. As she lay down alongside me, I realized she'd grabbed another ice cube as she ran it up my arm and across my chest ending at my nipple, circling it. In response, it puckered and heightened my need for her to play with me.

"Please. Mistress." I could hear how desperate I sounded and didn't care. I was desperate. The sensation play from earlier mixed with this left me needy and wanting. The ice moved on to my other nipple leaving a trail of wetness and cold in its wake. As she tortured one to stiffness, though, her hot mouth engulfed the other breast and once again I was trying to process both intense heat and intense cold at the same time. It captured all of my attention and I moaned loudly.

"That's my good girl. Let me hear you." She brought the ice cube back to my hot nipple but this time enclosed it and my nipple with her mouth swirling the cold cube with her tongue.

I was so engrossed in what was happening with my breast, it took me a minute to register that her hand was between my legs. She speared her fingers into me as she bit down on my overly sensitized nipple and I wailed, "Aaaahh!" And then gasped out, "Oh. I. Uh. Please." I'm not sure what I gasped out, but it wasn't coherent. Just a general plea for her to take care of me and my overwhelming pleasure.

"I have you, love." She reassured me, knowing what I needed without me having to say it. Her fingers pumped into me as her mouth found my other breast, the ice cube melted by now. I loved the way her curves pinned me to the bed. When she finally left my breast and pressed her lips to mine, I moaned into our kiss. It felt like it went on forever. Her hand was relentless the whole time, adding her thumb at my clit and as low in my belly, everything coiled in pleasure. I realized I couldn't catch a breath. She was kissing the very air out of me and it just ratcheted up my sensations even more. It was so overwhelming something was going to have to give.

It did. She released my mouth as her fingers wiggled on my g-spot and with my first gasp of full oxygen, I lost all control. After all the build-up, I screamed, I shook, and I came hard. "Holy hell! What was that?" I managed to say while still panting for air.

She wrapped me in her arms, and rolled over so I was laying with my head pillowed on her breast, cuddled to her side. "That, my love, was *very* satisfying indeed. My curiosity about the costumes can wait now."

"I totally forgot about the costumes. I think I forgot my name. I think I'd like to explore sensation play again in the future, because wow." I was blown away. My whole body was tingling.

"That was very enjoyable. I can't wait to play even more with it." She was so contented that I heard her heart rate change as she drifted off for a nap.

Pleasure of a different kind suffused my body knowing whatever had her a bit on edge before had left the building. This was something that I could give her and myself. I fell asleep but a minute later, plan stress all forgotten for now.

5

STICKY SITUATIONS

Lisa

FOUR DAYS LEFT before the party and my anxiety was about to hit a new critical level, "Tell me you're joking Tabitha. Please." I could hear the desperation in my voice. *Ugh!* I was supposed to already have the ring by now.

"I wish I was. The engraver had come back and made great strides working on your ring, but came down with something and couldn't come in today. Maybe it will be a twenty-four-hour thing and she'll be able to make up the time." She was trying to be optimistic but I could hear her desperation, too. "I will stay in close touch with the artist and let you know. I'm so sorry."

I knew my frustration wasn't going to change anything and it was all beyond Tabitha's control, but I wanted to scream. It was such a challenge, but I said, "I know. It's no one's fault. Hopefully, she can still make it happen while I figure out a plan b. Maybe Camila will find it romantic if I put a frisky bean donut on her finger."

"That sounds messy. Zero out of ten, do not recommend. I'll see what I can do, but I have to run. I have a meeting starting soon. Try to stay positive."

Positive. I called Alex to check on the flower headband they were making. That would make me feel better, right? "Hi, Alex. I'm calling to check—"

Over the phone, I heard, "Did I say you could touch the phone darling?" in someone else's voice. It was followed by Alex saying, "No. I was trying to shut it off. I'm sorry. How may I make it up to you?" *Did they not realize they'd answered my call?* The other person said, "You can lean over my lap and—" *Nope!* I slammed my finger into the disconnect call button so hard, I'm surprised I didn't break the glass or my finger. They clearly had no idea they'd answered the call. Checking on my order would have to wait. One more thing on my to-do list, not done. *Gah.*

I deserved a baked good and some coffee after the morning I'd had. After a quick text to Camila so she'd join me between lessons, I was off to The Frisky Bean. I didn't even have to walk in before the scent of pure joy caused my mouth to water. Kevin Johnson, the head baker and co-owner of the café, was the one at the register which was very unusual. "Hey, Kevin. It's not often I get to see you outside of your kingdom." I waved toward the door to the kitchen.

"Too true, but Summer went over to Alex's shop to discuss some final arrangements for the party so I'm filling in—why are you laughing?"

"I don't think Summer is going to get the details she was going for, but she will get something out of the encounter."

"Oh, honey. Do tell." Kevin leaned forward on the counter like a coconspirator, but just then the door behind me opened and when I turned to see who it was, there stood Summer.

She tiptoed for some reason up to us and said quietly for no one else to here, "Alex closed the shop early today but forgot to, um, close the door. They were with Ash doing what those two enjoy together that didn't involve flowers, stores, or me. Oh, wait. No. I guess there was a flower but I don't think we should talk about it. But also, bravo to Ash for her creativity with flora." That was when she took note of me standing there and said, "Lisa! Has Kevin given you our latest treat we're testing for the party and for our Matanot L'evyonim? We're organizing with Benny, who is a leader within the local home-less community, to hand out all our gift boxes of food on that day."

"I love that you are doing that! Let me know if I can help in any way. But, no, Kevin hasn't. I walked in maybe a minute before you. Of course, I didn't get to see anything as exciting as you did..." I waggled my eyebrows at her and continued, "I would love to try it— the treat, not whatever Ash had done with the flower. Or, maybe I do? Hmm... I might need to learn more about this."

Kevin had a plate with another Hamantaschen in front of me. This one, like all of them, was made in the traditional triangle shape but had some sort of white and brown—"Is that burnt marshmallow?"

He answered, "Lisa. Meet the Give Me S'more Hamantaschen. Made with the same flavors other people remember from camping while I remember them from theme night fun with Nana Vera. You're going to love it."

I put the dessert up to my mouth and could smell the chocolate underneath the fluff. Decadent. But, if I thought it looked and smelled great, it was nothing compared with how it tasted. Around my first bite, I might have made some very inappropriate sounds, but it was *that* good.

I vaguely registered the door opening again. "May I join you two? You and whatever is in your mouth that is." Camila came up and took a bite of my dessert from what was left in my hand. After her own inappropriate moment, she purred, "I am down for this threeway."

As I contemplated licking a sticky combination of marshmallow fluff and chocolate drizzle from her perky breasts, I saw Kevin and Summer high-fiving each other. Summer was the one who spoke, though, "I think our work here is done." Kevin disappeared into the kitchen. Summer busied herself behind the counter. Camila and I took turns finishing our 'taschen while never losing eye contact.

"It's nice to see you during the day. Are you meeting a client here?" She casually leaned on the counter as she asked.

"No. Not today. I was in dire need of caffeine and baked goods. What would you like to get?" I reached out and held her hand in both of mine. "Do you want your usual Tempt Me Tea? Iced?" I brought her fingers to my mouth and kissed them. The way her eyes dilated, I knew she, too, remembered what I had done with ice recently. "Maybe with a little sweetness?" I kissed the inside of her wrist. "Perhaps they could pour some honey on…ehem…in it." I kissed the tip of her pointer finger. "Perhaps we could share a Pinch Me Poached Pear Pocket?" I kissed the top of her wrist. Her breathing was growing more ragged by the minute.

Camila licked her lips. I subtly licked the inside of her wrist as I kissed it again. I was going to need to reign it in, but she was so temptingly alert. I pulled her in and placed a kiss on her forehead and simply held her for a minute. I did some deep breathing and she joined me, syncing our breaths to relax. I leaned down and whispered in her ear, "Good girl." Still holding her, I felt her instant reaction to my praise. I also felt when she shook it off.

We turned to the counter to place an order and Kevin and Summer were standing there with love-struck, goofy faces on them. I should probably feel embarrassed for all the PDA, but all I felt was pleased. Summer spoke and the tension was completely broken.

"Now I've seen two Frisky Bean couples sexing each other up within less than fifteen minutes. I need to call Jason." With that, she walked into the back.

Kevin, having returned, spoke next, "Man. I miss the boyfriend I had in my teen years. You remind me of him a little bit, Camila. He was so beautiful. Ah… First crushes are hard to get over. Since you've left Summer unable to function, can I get you something?"

Spending even a short time with Camila before she had to go back to work had done wonders for my anxiety. The problem was, as soon as she left and I was alone, it all came rushing back.

6

A COUPLE OF QUEENS

Camila

I DON'T KNOW how people do this. *How do people organize things?* I had lists upon lists to try to keep track of everything and I had to hide those lists so Lisa wouldn't find them. Summer and I had worked out all the details of when it would happen, how we were going to arrange for us both to be on the "stage" at the same time, and Lisa's favorite dessert to be served right after to celebrate. I had the costumes and accompanying jewelry, I had little streamers for friends to throw around us, and I of course had the ring. *I did have the ring, right?* I checked my purse for the twentieth time to make sure it was there. Still good.

Okay.

Everything was okay.

Honestly, it's a bit shocking that I was able to keep all of this from Lisa. Of course, Lisa hadn't been around or available that much in the last few days. In truth, it was starting to worry me. She seemed stressed but she kept assuring me that she was fine. We've always been able to talk about anything. For her to be keeping something from me was weird. Of course, I was keeping something from her, so it would be hard to complain. After tonight's party, though, she and I were going to need to talk.

Thinking of what we might be doing after the party made me amend it to tomorrow morning. I was so deep in thought about the evening, that I squealed when Lisa's arms surrounded me from behind. She put her chin on my shoulder and said, "Hi, love."

"Hi!" I spun in her arms and was taken aback a bit by how she looked. My fashionista had her hair the messiest I'd seen outside of the bedroom. Even her clothes and jewelry seemed askew. The most concerning was that her eyes seemed slightly dulled somehow. This was supposed to be such a happy day, but wasn't sure she was in the mood for what I had planned.

"Are you still okay with going tonight?"

It was so clear she was working hard to pull herself together on the fly, and it must have succeeded because she seemed in a little less of a bad mood as she answered. "You know how stressed I've been about my new client, but I want to go tonight. I'll rally as I put on my costume. Do you mind sharing what I'm wearing, finally?"

"Greta Garbo." I'd grabbed her attention with that pronouncement. "You are Greta and I'm her notorious girlfriend Mercedes de Acosta. Together we are scandalous." I winked and ran to the bedroom to bring out the costumes. She followed behind me and when I pulled out the gorgeous, slinky, sequined, blue gown with a rope of pearls necklace to go with it, her eyes shifted from tired to glittering.

"That's...Stunning! I can't wait to put it on. Oh! And, I have the perfect makeup to go with it. And, of course, I'm going to need to do my hair a little differently. This is perfect!"

She grabbed me up into a bear hug and gave me a solid kiss on the lips before setting me down. She looked poised to run off but then remembered she hadn't seen what I was wearing yet. After she mouthed the word, "Sorry," I pulled out my clothes which consisted of a stiff but loose, boxy black dress with a fancy, dangling belt rope in gold and decorative sequined-lace panels that extended from the shoulders to the elbows.

She gasped, "I can't wait to see you in it. This is so fun. Thank you for taking care of it!"

I basically beamed in return. "My pleasure!"

Lisa decided it would be fun to get ready separately, so I chose to get ready in the family room and she got ready in the bedroom. I had sewn a hidden pocket into my dress earlier in the week, when she had been out, and had the ring stored safely there.

"Did you invite Rabbi Ruth to the party?" Lisa yelled from the bedroom in a joking tone.

"You joke, but I *had* invited her. She said she would have to let me know, and I haven't heard from her, so it's probably unlikely but not out of the realm of possibility."

"I hope she can. I know you got close during your conversion classes."

"Yes, but not as close as you and I got while mingling at the oneg after Shabbat services." I was tempted to go into the bedroom since I was already done getting ready, but I reminded myself to be good. Lisa wanted us both surprised at the same time.

"I recall bonding over a particularly tasty chocolate halva babka that someone was kind enough to bring. I'm almost ready. I'll be out soon." Her words sounded weird and I realized she must be applying lipstick which is one of the last things she puts on.

"That was a great babka. I never did get that recipe. Pity. You and I have been bonding over baked goods and are still keeping up that tradition by meeting up at The Frisky Bean all the time." I sat on the couch on my hands to once again remind myself not to go into the bedroom. She would come out soon.

Like I had conjured her, there she was. Walking down the hall was a vision of glamorous Hollywood. I jumped to my feet and stumbled my way to stand in front of her to take her all in. The dress hugged every one of her luscious curves and I wanted to rip it off of her and see her only in the long rope of pearls I had gotten her and the pearly white heels she had paired the outfit with. She was still the most beautiful thing I'd ever seen. "The dress on the hanger could never do justice to how it looks on you. You make a stunning Greta."

She reached out and tilted my chin on the crook of her finger. "And you, my dear, make a beautiful Mercedes. Do you plan to write me a poem? Maybe a play?"

Considering I kind of had written something for her today, I had to contain my panic and quietly said, "Too busy tonight, but check with me in the morning. There's this gorgeous blond who has stolen my heart and I can't be distracted with words. But, by morning...who knows? Maybe I'll write a poem about her lips if I get lucky tonight."

"She'd be a fool if she doesn't come home with you tonight. Would you really have fallen for a fool? I think not, so I'm pretty sure she's a sure thing. But, for now, we have to get going. We don't want to be late." She gave me a quick peck on the lips and then gathered her pearl-adorned clutch.

A picture of someone perfectly put together, but I could still sense some tension. Perhaps in her shoulders? "Everything okay?"

"Absolutely. Let's go." Out we went, but if I was honest, her weird stress of late was contagious and I felt I was starting to come down with some myself.

7

COSTUMES, CACOPHONY, AND
CHAOS

Lisa

WE ARRIVED at The Frisky Bean and I was filled with so much excitement and so much frustration. I was going to have to propose with an aluminum foil ring I crafted in Summer's kitchen or something. Tabitha had kept me informed every day about the progress but with delay after delay, she finally had to inform me that they had been close but were not going to be able to give me the ring. That had been this morning and I'd been carrying around a cloak of sadness ever since. It was *not* going to derail my intentions for the evening, but it would make it not perfect. I suppose there's a grudging lesson in there about trying to reach perfection.

I held tight to the philosophical approach for all of a minute before I excused myself to the restroom. I needed an excuse to sneak into the kitchen and find a quiet space to wave at my definitely not-leaking eyes to un-moisten them. That was how Summer found me fanning my own face.

"Is everything okay?" she asked full of concern.

"Yes." The fact that I had to fan even faster to keep my face non-wet was fine too.

"Does this have something to do with the big ask? Because you know Camila is totally a sure thing. You two are my couple goals." She came up and wrapped an arm around me and I may have had to wipe at a stray not-tear that hadn't rolled down my cheek.

"I didn't get the ring in time. You wouldn't happen to have a spare engagement ring that looks like the one I commissioned lying around, do you?" I meant it as a joke, but don't think I sounded too convincing.

"Can't say that I do, but I'm sure even if you give it to her another time it will be okay. She won't care."

"I know you're right. I don't know why I am getting so emotional about the damn ring. It'll be fine. Okay. Thank you for the not-a-pep-talk since I obviously did not need one. And, sorry about sneaking into your kitchen. Nice costume by the way...very old school. Queen Esther right?"

Summer joyfully exclaimed, "Bullseye. It's our first Purim here so I had to go traditional. Next year, who knows."

We parted and I found Camila talking to Alex and Ash. The latter was dressed as one of the *Men in Black* operatives and Alex was the alien Leeloo from the movie *Fifth Element*. They looked so cute together.

I joined the group as Ash was saying, "I love Purim. Getting to celebrate a Mizrachi queen who saved her people is a holiday that speaks to my soul. When I was growing up, I loved helping my mom cook and organize the gift baskets full of yummy treats to send mishloach manot to every family in our small Bene Israel community and beyond. Being a detail-oriented person, it was both fun and good preparation for the parties I throw today."

"I love that tradition as well," Camila exclaimed. "I find such peace as I work on putting them together, knowing they bring people so much joy. Speaking of... Something may or may not be arriving tomorrow." She winked at the couple.

Alex winked back. "Right back at you."

Someone in the room started to yell, "Haman," but before they could get through the second syllable, we all raised whatever noise-maker we'd picked up on the way in and the room broke out in a cacophony, drowning out the antagonist's name from the Purim story.

As things settled back down, Ash and Camila were chatting excitedly about potentially doing one of Ash's influencer parties at the yoga studio and what that might look like. Alex used the opportunity to pull me aside with what I hoped was good news. *But do you ever pull people aside with good news? Maybe?*

"I'm so sorry, Lisa. I know you wanted a crown of spray roses in light purple with some lavender, but the shipment of fresh spray roses never arrived. I was on the phone with them all day yesterday and they assured me they would arrive today, but never did. They don't know where they've ended up. I still have a beautiful crown for you, unfortunately, it's just lavender. I added some ribbon and it's truly lovely, but—"

They looked so concerned I couldn't let them keep fretting over it, so I said, "It's okay. I'm sure the lavender will be beautiful. Thank you for letting me know." *Why was nothing going as planned?* I am meticulous dangit. And for the most important thing I've done so far in my life, I couldn't seem to do any of it right. I don't have the ring. The flower crown isn't her favorite flower. The universe was mocking me. Camila deserved perfection.

I hadn't noticed that I'd been twisting at my necklace in frustration, but I did when I looked over at my love and found her looking at me with concern. Our eyes met and she looked about to ask me something but stopped. If I had to guess, it was inquiring once again if I was okay and the answer was no...yes...maybe? I should be okay. It's all so silly to get upset about, but I was feeling more and more out of control and I didn't like it. Camila grabbed my hand which was when

I noticed I had switched from twirling my necklace to twirling my finger into the fabric of my dress.

"Please excuse us." Camila deftly extricated us from the conversation and despite our normal dynamic, pushed me very successfully through the crowd and into one of the unisex bathrooms. "What is going on with you? And I won't take 'everything is fine' as your answer so try again."

I don't think I'd ever seen her so fired up and commanding before. It was impossible for me not to notice how beautiful she was even while annoyed with me. But, how could I tell her what's wrong without telling her what my plan was for tonight? "I'll tell you later, I promise."

"What's wrong with now?" She even folded her arms angrily.

I was making things go from not perfect to bad. "I would prefer to talk about it later. I think we should enjoy the holiday, our friends, and the night. Could we do that?" I put a hand on her folded arms trying to bridge the gulf I'd created. "Please."

I could see when she softened to my request. Her arms loosened and she held my hand to her chest. "Will you be able to enjoy tonight with whatever is on your mind still bothering you?"

"Yes. I was having a moment, but you're so right. I need to realign my priorities and for tonight all of them are you." I pulled her in for a hug and simply held her close for a bit. With a deep breath to center my focus, I was back to me. I would pivot with whatever came, and one way or another, I would ask this amazing partner of mine to marry me before the night was through. I had been so focused on the wrong things going right. *This* was right, right here. "Thank you. I needed that. I love you, you know."

"Oh. I know," she said snarkily as she turned out of my arms to grab the door.

I swatted her ass for that remark and hauled her back to me with my hand gently cradling her throat. With my mouth right at her ear, I hissed, "Is that all you have to say to me?"

"Oh. I know... Mistress." I couldn't help it. She got me. I snickered.

"Fine. You don't have to say it back. I love you. I love you. I love you. And you know what? I know you love me too." I gently bit down on her ear as a little reminder and then let go so we could exit the room.

She looked over her shoulder briefly and said, "I do," before opening the door and walking out.

PURIM PROPOSAL SPIEL

Camila

COSTUME CONTEST TIME! I watched as all the contestant solos, groups, and couples went up for everyone to see. We were fast approaching our turn. Summer, Kevin, and I planned it so that we were the last ones called up. Kevin was MCing and the party, ever since our conversation in the bathroom, was a lot of fun. Rabbi Ruth had indeed shown up and was mingling with some customers I'd never met before and some I had. One of those couples was Tabitha, someone Lisa worked closely with, and her fiancé Sean. They were dressed as *Mr. and Mrs. Smith*. They literally wore t-shirts that labeled them as such. Not a lot of effort but cute nonetheless.

We'd also had a chance to talk to Jason and Summer earlier and her roommate Jessica as well. There were other folks around that I'd met at the café and everyone was having a good time. The hamantaschen were a hit and moods were high—the perfect setting for a joyous proposal.

And then Kevin called our names and we were heading to the

stage. It was weird though. Alex stopped Lisa along the way and seemed to hand her something. We walked up and we had people try to guess who we were, but no one got it exactly right. Instead of confessing who we were, I put my hand in my pocket, ready to extract the ring box and get down on one knee. Before I could, I found a crown of lavender placed on my head and Lisa knelt before me.

She was about to talk and I blurted, "Wait. I was supposed to do that."

Her look of confusion was comical except I was the one who felt lost in the script.

She sounded as confused as she looked when she said, "I'm trying to propose here if you don't mind."

"Well, I do mind." Her look of horror made me realize how that sounded so I rushed to add, "I'm proposing to you right now!" I went down on one knee and showed her the ring box.

So many feelings passed over her face from joyful to sad. Why was she sad? It kind of, maybe irked me a step too much. Making a plan may not be my forte, but I had one for tonight and nothing was going to get in my way. I just needed to get the paper with my poem from my pocket and—

Just then, a commotion began at the back and we could hear someone yelling, "I've got it! I've got it!"

The crowd started jovially chanting for no apparent reason, "She's got it. She's got it. Oh, baby, she's got it," from that old eighties song, "Venus."

"For the love of coffee, will someone please tell me what's going on? I'm in the middle of something here. I had plans you know?"

Lisa reached for my hand, "You had plans? *I* had plans!"

Meanwhile, the woman yelling, "I've got it," made it to the front of the crowd and slapped a box into Lisa's other hand. She yelled again, "We did it!" and then proceeded to do a victory lap.

"That was Tabitha, right?" I watched as she high-fived Sean.

"Why is she victorious while I'm trying to propose to you?" I had a poem to read and everything.

Lisa flipped open her box, diverting my attention back to her, and inside lay the most beautiful ring I'd ever seen. It was wide silver with intricate engravings that reminded me of... "Oh, my G! It is just like my great-grandma's ring! It's so beautiful!" I threw my arms around Lisa and yelled, "Yes!"

"I haven't asked you anything yet," she laughed as she held me close. "But, you can't take it back." I leaned back and she slipped the ring onto my finger which was when I realized that there were also rings around the wide band that were free-floating. I automatically began spinning them with my thumb.

"You got me a fidget toy!"

"Yep."

I threw my arms around her again. The way that this woman got me... she was my everything. "Thank you! It's so beautiful! Now sit back and let me do what I came here to do."

From the same pocket that held the ring, I pulled out the paper I had written my poem on and began to read.

> "Lisa, my love, you make my heart sing.
> So after much searching, I found this ring.
> A symbol of our hands joined together
> Holding our combined love and light forever."

I opened the box and nestled inside was an heirloom ring I'd scoured the internet to find: two hands twisted around and holding an aquamarine which reminded me of Lisa's eye color. She studied it with tears in her eyes, not that she would admit they were there.

I realized I hadn't asked her either so to make it official, I said, "Will you marry me?"

"Yes! Your poem was beautiful and this ring, I have no words except I love you and yes!"

I slipped the ring on her finger to the cheers of everyone. We hugged and shed absolutely no tears. Nope. None at all. After using the many tissues people handed us, we stood up and faced the crowd. Everyone tossed the streamers I'd provided in our direction and we were officially engaged.

Lisa, accusingly but with good humor, pointed at Summer and Kevin and said, "You! You knew all along about both of us I assume?"

Without even thinking about it, they both answered at the same time, "Definitely."

Rabbi Ruth was the first to come and congratulate us. "If you happen to need a Rabbi to officiate, I may know a gal who would love that." She nudged each of us playfully and said her goodbyes.

Everyone in the room came by to congratulate us, whether we knew them or not, and the evening began to wind down.

Amongst all the commotion I'd forgotten about the costume contest, so I asked Kevin who won. One of the customers had dressed up as an obscure reference to an Alexis Hall novel by wearing an Arnold Palmer costume, a rose clip in his hair, and walking around with a cake. For all of us romance readers in the room, we got it, and I was glad to hear he'd won. Especially considering we were the real winners of the night.

I brought our joint hands up and kissed Lisa's knuckles. It was time to shed these costumes.

9

TURNABOUT IS PLAY

Lisa

I HONESTLY COULD NOT HAVE PREDICTED any of what happened tonight except one thing. Camila said yes and that was all that mattered. She's been the love of my heart and soul almost from the beginning. Having reached the other side of events, I can't believe how much stress I caused us both over things that, in the end, were so insignificant compared to our love.

We arrived at our apartment, and as soon as I got her inside, I had to get this off my chest. "I'm so sorry. I'm sorry that I worried you even for a minute. I'm sorry I let all the things going wrong sour my celebrating all the things going right until you called me on my bull-shit. I love you so much and I wanted you to have the perfect proposal."

"I gathered as much by the end of the evening. Don't get me wrong, I love my ring, and I love the flower crown, but all I needed was you and you said yes. Perfect." It was rare that she initiated actual sexual contact, but she chose this time to be an exception. She leaned into me as I stood in front of the closed door and planted her lips on mine, her body on mine. Showing me how much she valued us through intimacy.

It was bound to be for only a short time, and it was. I flipped our positions around, trapping her against the door, lifted my dress off of one of my legs, and notched that knee between her thighs. "Ride my thigh."

She rubbed her pussy on me while I undid her belt, throwing the dress over her head and off. She was down to a demi-bra and a scrap of lace between her legs that was soaked and needed to go. I had other plans. I kissed her, tracing my fingers along the edges of her bra. Teasing. Tempting. Maybe a little bit tormenting even. She arched her back in an attempt to get me to do more, but I kept stroking at the lacy border.

Camila grew frenzied in my arms, which is when I cupped her breast fully and pinched her nipple. She cried out even as her body arched deeper into my palm. I played with her tits for a long time until they were hard points and the lightest touch brought torturous moans from her lips. Meanwhile, I made sure the friction of her pussy rubbing against my thigh wasn't enough for her to come. She was strung tight and on the edge.

Breathtaking.

I watched her for a moment longer luxuriating in having the control firmly back where I was most comfortable, with me. She was able to let go with full abandon and was going to enjoy what I planned next. I kissed her deeply one more time, and when I came up for air, I ordered her to finish stripping and then position herself leaning over the dining table, legs spread.

I admit that I reconsidered briefly since conventional thought said we should be making sweet love. We *had* just gotten engaged, after all. But, I thought back to the conversation in The Frisky Bean kitchen and about the way she smirked devilishly when I promised her a spanking and knew that conventional wasn't our path. We were who we were. After our wild night, we could both use the release.

Regardless, I looked for any indication that she wasn't in the mood to play, but all I could see was eagerness in every line of her bent body. Our time together had taught us to read each other's clues without having to say a word.

She had the most beautiful ass. My fingers tingled with the anticipation to touch her. Then they tingled for a whole other reason. The first smack took her by surprise and had her yelping, "Hey!"

"Earlier, was that you refusing to admit your love for me?" *Smack.*

Of course, she chose not to fess up to it right away. What would be the fun in that?

"Maybe? There was so much going on, it's hard to—Uhhh" *Smack.* She grunted. Probably because I made that one sting a bit. We both knew that after the sting came the heat and sure enough, it took no time for her to start wiggling her butt silently asking for more.

"I distinctly remember the exchange. Need me to read the official transcripts?" *Smack.*

"No," she whimpered. "I recall. I'm sorry and I love you sooooooo much."

"Are you mocking me?" *Smack.* "You realize if you want it, you could just ask for it, right?" I caressed her reddened butt cheeks. "Have you learned your lesson?"

She thought about it for a few seconds and said, "I don't think I have."

If she was game for more, then so was I. I would never tire of bringing her pleasure. *My gorgeous girl.*

Smack. Smack. Smack.

She was panting by the third one. I caressed the heat into her skin and her panting became a long moan. "Yes. Feel me. Your friend. Your lover. Your bashert. I love you so much."

Swiftly she replied, "I love you too. You are my very lifeblood."

"Let's move this to the bedroom." I helped her, from behind, back to a standing position. She groaned again as her stiff nipples stopped being smooshed against the wood table. Her body leaned into mine, letting me support her, as she got her bearings. I kissed her neck and plucked at her tortured peaks. "You are so lovely like this. Flushed, sensitive, and so open to me."

When she was able to stand on her own, she turned toward me and whispered sweetly, "Can I make a request?"

I interlocked our left hands and lifted them, awed anew at the joint rings on them. My voice was full of emotions when I replied, "Anything."

"Can we do more experiments with ice?"

"Caught a thrill for temperature play? Well, you're not alone. Yes. I'll grab the ice, you grab my red... no, make it my lavender strap-on and the lube. It's a night for new adventures, don't you think?" I pulled her in for a kiss before she left.

At the door, she turned and said, "Life with you is always full of new adventures, my love."

"Thank you for choosing to take that journey with me."

"I love you."

"I know."

I could hear her incredulous laugh the whole way down the hall.

I looked down at the ring one more time and counted myself thoroughly blessed.

EXCERPT FROM FRISKY CONNECTIONS

Chapter 1

"Really. It's fine, honey. You couldn't have predicted a bird bombing as soon as you stepped out of the house. I'd turn right around and need a shower too." Shira Abramson spoke into her phone, tempering her disappointment and comforting her friend Keren Sabinski once again.

As her friend apologized for the hundredth time, she returned, "I *know* you'd come if you could. We both knew this was going to have to be a quick get together as it was."

Keren finally said, "I know. I know. It's just that I was so fucking excited to see you. It's been too long. I feel sooo bad. And instead of girl chat, I get to remove bird shit from my hair. Ew."

"I think I come out just fine compared to you, so don't worry even for a second. I'll just grab a quick coffee and get some work done. No biggie."

"Actually, if you still plan to grab a coffee, might I suggest you try out my company's new app?"

"Which app?"

"Immedia-Date."

"The dating app you described to me last month?"

"Yep. The very one. It's just come out this week and we've already had a ton of people sign up. Give it a try. Maybe you'll meet Mr. Right today and shitting birds will have a silver lining. It would be good for your blog *and* you can provide me with feedback."

"You're such a yenta."

"I'll wear that matchmaking badge with pride, thank you very much. Yenta heart. Business brain. Now give it a go, and I'm going to wash my hair a million times over and then head to my meeting."

"Fine. If I end up dead in a ditch somewhere, I'll know who to blame." Shira grumbled.

"Enjoy. Avoid the ditch. Text your bitch. That sounded a lot better in my head than out loud. You know what I mean, though. Text me when you're done. Bye."

With that, the line went dead.

What had she just agreed to? Shira opened up the app store and searched for Immedia-Date. She located it and had it downloaded quickly. She was impressed right away with the ease of setting it up. The streamlined process was a snap. Answer a few simple questions and it created a basic profile with what you were looking for. Tall, dark, Jewish a bonus, and handsome a desire. The app prompted that all she needed to do now, was turn her profile to 'currently available' and it would search her vicinity for any available matches interested in a short pop-up date. So she did just that. Easy peasy.

Her phone dinged almost right away, making her jump. Someone was available and interested in meeting up with her. *Well, that was fast.*

She opened the app back up, clicked on the profile of the interested party, and had to blink a few times. This had to be a scam. No one joined a dating app and got one of the hottest guys she'd ever seen in the first couple of minutes. She bet it was someone catfishing with a fake picture, but that could be resolved quickly when they met, so she clicked "Interested." The app took a minute to search the area between them for a highly rated coffee shop or café within a short distance.

Her phone dinged again with the address to the shop. Shira figured she would at least discover a new place to get her caffeine fix out of this ill-advised adventure into modern dating. Coffee was life, after all. She pulled out of the parking lot where she had meant to meet Keren and headed to her Immedia-Date with some trepidation laced with excitement.

She arrived a few minutes later at her destination and was intrigued by the place right away. She checked out the map on the app and her date was still a few minutes away, so she decided to investigate the place on her own. The front window boasted a sign that read:

Welcome to The Frisky Bean
Coffee to Wake You Up
Pastries to Turn You On

Shira was now more than intrigued. What kind of crazy coffee place was this? And was it really appropriate for a first date? She shrugged and stepped inside. Right away, she realized she didn't care. The scents in this café made her mouth water, and she nearly moaned out loud in pleasure. Well, damn. New favorite café indeed.

"Hi there! Welcome to The Frisky Bean. Have you been here before? Probably not, since I'd remember if you had and of course we've only been open for eight months, so quite new. What can I get for you?"

This was all said with such speed and exuberance, Shira nearly flinched. She had to wonder if this could still be her favorite new place with the overly cheery person working behind the counter. Was there a way to maybe avoid her? Order ahead? Her consternation with being overwhelmed with perkiness must have shown on her face because the woman with the stunning, messy, curly red hair grimaced and said with less exuberance, "Too much, huh?" Her voice dropped to nearly a whisper. "Sorry. You're obviously one of the people who needs some coffee defenses before I approach you. Let's try that again." And with a dramatically less excited almost comically even tone she said, "Is there something I can help you with?"

Comical it might be, but it worked. Shira was now ready to answer. "Sorry. Coffee first may as well be my motto, but so should, Oscar the Grouch was misunderstood." She winked, hoping to diffuse the tension she'd accidentally created. It seemed to have worked, as the woman behind the counter visibly relaxed. So she continued: "I'm meeting someone here. They should be arriving any minute. Do you have a menu I can look at until then?"

"Sure." The woman handed her a card and then continued, still in a friendly but calm tone, "My name is Summer. Let me know when you're ready to order."

"Thanks."

"No problem. Take your time."

As she perused the menu, Shira's eyes opened wide and she felt a blush creeping up her cheeks. That slogan on the window wasn't kidding around. A bell sounded behind her, but she was so engrossed in the menu items, she forgot to keep a look out for her date. She was oblivious until she heard a deep, sexy male voice coming from right next to her. "See something you like?" In fact, it came from too close. She reacted before she could think better of it, leaving her full of regrets the moment after.

EXCERPT FROM FRISKY INTENTIONS

Chapter 1 - Keys, Part One

Summer

"Oh my god. That's so good." I moaned, swiping at the cream escaping my mouth. "You gave me a mouthgasm."

"Don't I always?"

"Yes, yes you do."

"Yes I do, now get your ass in gear, because we only have time for a quickie this morning."

I took one more bite of the decadent new confection, pointedly ignoring my best friend and co-owner of our cafe, Kevin Johnson. Unlike what my Mama taught me, I spoke around my mouthful of sweet, delectable mana.

"If you wanted me to be quick, you shouldn't have handed me such taste-bud-stroking goodness as soon as I walked in the kitchen."

I cringed at his downright insulted look.

"Summer Palmer, it's like you don't even know me. When have I ever done anything less than a full, sensual, enticement of the senses?

I'm not risking the wrath of your Nana Winnie. That woman taught us well, and there's no way I'd insult her by doing anything 'just good.' You know she always said—"

I joined in with him reciting what Nana Winnie had taught us. I couldn't resist. "Food is love, and baked food is love with a kiss." Nana was so right. I felt it every time I got to baking. That special connection between me and the person enjoying my efforts filled me with all the best feels. I knew Kevin felt the exact same way. It's why we worked so well together.

Annnnnd... since he had a point, I tipped my head in agreement and apology. This was our dream after all. Each day that I stepped into the kitchen with Kevin and was enveloped by the scent of warm baked goodness, I was transported back to when we were kids. We'd spent endless hours learning from Nana Winnie. That quality and diligence showed in our relatively new café doing as well as it was. Uncontrollably moaning—again—around the last bite of our new pastry, the Pucker Cream Puff, nicknamed PCP because it was life altering, I washed my hands and set myself to doing some actual work.

As I chopped, I attempted to stay on task, but my mind kept wandering. Utterly unacceptable. Uneven fruit bits in the Feisty Fruit Cups would not pass my quality inspection, but despite my best efforts, I continued struggling to stay focused. I kept thinking back to the Goddess card I'd pulled that morning and what it could mean for my day.

I have this ritual, you see. Every morning, while getting ready, I pull a Goddess card for a daily spiritual guidance. It's been an important part of my routine for years. The cards never let me down. In fact, I credited them with helping me manifest the café.

That day, six months earlier, Kevin and I had gone to lunch for a preliminary discussion about our mutual dream. On the way back to the car, we'd walked past a store front with a lease sign. My card from that morning, which had given me the push to jump in, was the Greek Goddess Eos. Eos represents new beginnings, lust, and adventure. Since I'd learned to listen to my cards—and so had Kevin—we'd called and started the process to lease, on the spot. A short time later, The Frisky Bean went from dream to reality. And, here we were.

That same oh-so-powerful card was the one causing me so much emotional turmoil. Last time, I'd already been thinking about a transition so all I'd felt was excitement. But, getting such a powerful, life altering card on a random day? I wasn't prepared for any more life altering. I was still too busy with my previously altered life as it was. In the deep recesses of my mind, a new idea was poking at me, but no way was I ready for *that*. Life was good. I wouldn't want anything to risk destabilizing it. Goosebumps rose on my arms even as butterflies played in my stomach. Was I ready? I really didn't—

"Oh, shit! Motherfucker!"

I booked it to the nearest sink, threw the knife in, and quickly engulfed my finger in cold water.

Kevin rushed over, concern clear on his face and in his tone. "What the hell happened?"

"I won the lottery. What do you think happened? I cut my finger off."

"Don't take that tone with me, you big baby. Now let me see it."

I held out my hand for his inspection as I looked away sure that part of my finger was going to be dangling there like some mob boss movie. "Is it bad? Am I losing a finger? Dammit! I'm losing a finger, aren't I?"

I felt the eyeroll coming off of Kevin's tone. "Hon, you're clearly losing something, but it isn't your finger. It's barely worse than a paper cut. You'll survive."

I dared to look at my mortal wound, and yeah, okay, it wasn't *that* bad. Losing a finger would have definitely been a change, but clearly this wasn't what the Goddess's guidance had been referring to. While I stared, transfixed, at the thin line of blood that appeared just at the tip of my index finger on my left hand, Kevin disappeared and reappeared with a Band-Aid from the medical kit in the office. He gently wrapped it around and I watched as my not-so-mortal wound disappeared.

"Wanna tell me why you're so distracted that you're cutting yourself? It isn't like you to be careless or graceless while we bake. Other times, absolutely. But here? No way. You look—" He gave me a once-over, "—anxious."

I considered his question and my answer as he turned away, washed his hands, and wandered back to his own work space. He continued his earlier preparations, scooping mounds of "Sultry" Snickerdoodles onto a baking sheet because nothing but a lost limb would distract him from a smooth-running kitchen. When it came to baking and business, Kevin was all schedules, game plans, and potentially baked-goodness-world-domination. Nothing would come between him and our success.

Also, as my childhood best friend, he knew when I needed my space, like right then. So, instead of pressing me for answers he went back to work and waited patiently.

I took the silent space he provided and continued to consider my answer while doing mindless tasks. I washed the knife twice in scorching water and carefully set it aside. Then, I cleaned up the whole station, sanitizing it and tossing potentially contaminated fruit away. Finally, after covering my injured hand with a glove, I kept on working. Seeing as how distraction got me injured in the first place, I wasn't ready to handle the knife just yet, so I grabbed some mandarin oranges, peeled and put a few slices into each cup. A safe part of my routine.

Thoughts collected, I started to explain in a rush of words, "I don't think anxious is quite right, but I'm not sure if I have a better word. I'm feeling...restless? Or maybe uncertain?"

Ugh! This was *sooo* not like me. *Get your shit together and stop being such a Nervous Nellie!* I took a slow, deep, calming breath and tried again.

"It's probably nothing. I'm not sure why I'm so weirded out, but do you remember that Goddess card I got the day we leased this place? Well, I got her today and I guess since I don't feel ready for any major upheavals right now," though my mind briefly alighted on that one new idea I'd been flirting with, "I'm all out of sorts. It's probably nothing."

There. That sounded almost coherent and like I was back to making sense.

I picked up the knife again, ready to tackle the rest of the fruit when Kevin scolded from across the kitchen, "If you're handling that knife again, you better fucking relax or you'll end up chopping the fruit into varying sizes or actually losing a finger. You know the first shit don't fly and the second will throw my baking schedule off for the whole day and that don't fly either. Anyway, you're probably right."

Kevin smirked while saying this which had me narrowing my eyes at him. Before I could inquire about that smirk, though, he continued, "Of course, maybe some hot guy will sweep you off your feet today. That would be a life change you could use. Hell, that would be a life change *I* could use. Could I get that card next?" His smirk turned wicked, "Maybe we could have a good ol' cat fight over today's hot lover?"

"Uh huh." I gave him my unamused face. Truth was, Kevin was a beautiful Black man. His arm muscles bunched beneath his tight t-shirt as he put the trays in the oven, taking out others that were ready. He looked like the love child of Blair Underwood and the Black Panther himself, Chadwick Boseman. Of medium height, dark, beautiful soulful eyes, and a smile for days. I would never want to compete with him for a man. No way would I win that battle.

Still, what kind of friend would I be if I let him throw down like that without dishing it right back? "You know I'd totally take you in that fight, right? I got my ninja skills on lockdown."

"Girl, you wouldn't even be able to get into a ninja outfit without falling down. I'm not even sure I'd have to fight you. You'd take two steps my way and knock yourself out on a counter."

Warmth suffused me, surely blotching my pale cheeks. Bantering with Kevin was one of my favorite pastimes. I lamented to him, while returning to my chopping, "Damn. It sucks when your friends know walking is your Achilles heel."

"Tabling the hot men for now—"

"Yes. Tables of hot men. I'll take that please."

"Quiet down hussy. As I was saying, all I have left after the cookies, is to cool the 3B and then work on some more muffins and scones. I made extra 3B since we've been running out of it lately. Who knew it would be our best seller? I guess after that Fifty Shades book everyone thinks they're into BDSM."

"Oh! That reminds me. I came up with a name for the almond coconut balls we've been planning. What do you think of Sweet Hairy Balls?" I waggled my eyebrows at him.

"I don't think I want to know how you came up with that. Or maybe I do. Either way, it's perfection. Who doesn't like some Sweet Hairy Balls?" He snorted. "I'll add those into the baking rotation starting tomorrow morning. Now back to business, lazy bones."

They settled into a companionable silence working side-by-side. Their morning prep was like a perfected ballet. All movement efficient, effective, and creating beauty. In their case, edible beauty. Baking was the only place that I ever felt graceful. I was usually tripping over my own feet—and had the bruises to prove it—but when I baked, somehow my mind shut down, the world receded, and I flowed. That was the best way I could describe it, and I craved the high it gave me regularly.

An hour later, I gazed at the tempting tray of completed 3B—or Bondage Banana Bread—our signature baked good. After the bread cooled, I'd sliced it and laid the pieces out in a single layer. Then, I wrapped thin strips of sugared banana around them and brûléed the banana onto the bread. I couldn't help the fact that my mouth watered every single time, and this time had been no different. They could be classified a dessert, they were so decadently delicious.

I picked up the finished tray and notified Kevin I was going to open. Pushing through the swinging kitchen door with my hip, I set the tray in the display case. With one last review of my comfortably small, beloved café, I made sure everything was ready to go. Warm and inviting as usual. The five rectangle-shaped tables with seating for two were all clean and orderly. In the two far corners, the comfy couches and chairs around low wood and metal tables were also neat and organized. All was in place.

I loved the ambiance we'd created with the warm mustard color we had chosen for the walls and even more so loved the pictures hanging there. They were provided by a local photographer, who preferred to remain anonymous, to showcase their work and sell them.

The images were black and white and suggestive. An obscure body part here, a rounded body part there. I found them evocative, classy, and also sexy as hell. Perfect for our theme and for my inner sex kitten, assuming I actually had one of those that is. I was no novice with my sexuality, but none of the guys I'd dated or slept with so far had ever fully done it for me. Sex was... mmm... okay, but I wanted so much more. I wanted fireworks. Maybe throw in some kink. Something. My toys had more game than the men I'd been dating lately.

In many ways, the theme of the café was my and Kevin's way of sending out into the universe a request for passion, since he felt much the same as I did. I hoped someones out there were listening. Maybe the Goddess was, like Kevin predicted, about a new relationship. Part of me was excited by the prospect and part of me didn't have time for anything else. After having a brief reprieve, finishing up my part of prepping, I was right back to distraction like I'd been earlier. With a wistful sigh, I made my way around the counter of the display case and unlocked the door, flipping the sign to open.

I turned to walk back and, "Dang it!" dropped my keys, because of course I did. In my frustration, I let out a low scream from between my teeth, as the keys loudly clattered to the floor. There was nothing for it. I leaned over to grab them and, of course, that's when I heard the door open behind me. Still bent over, realization that I'd given our first customer of the day quite the backside view struck me much like puberty did... embarrassingly. Mortified, I startled into action. Unfortunately, I swung up too fast and fell backward into whoever had come in. Strong arms wound around me and my breath caught even as my heart raced at the feel of muscles. Lots of yummy muscles and —*oh* my—heat. Heat that radiated from those arms straight into my torso, osmosis style. Somehow, that heat traveled south at warp speed.

"Oh, shit!" The words escaped before I could professionally temper them. So, of course, I stumbled over my words too, "I'm so, so sorry. I... I..." I grudgingly stepped out of the arms and spun. I planned to offer my apologies for the ass view, the falling, and the bad language. I planned to be a good store owner and make it up to whoever was there. I planned, and I failed, because when I got my first sight of the stranger, my jaw dropped low and the only thing that fell out was, "Holy, fuck!"

What. The. Hell? Summer!

Yes. That's right. That's what I said. And, clearly following the path paved in regrets I was on, I blushed, my blood rushing through my veins at an all too familiar pace, turning my face warm and blotchy, while a coppery taste entered my mouth. *Fuckity, fuck, fuck!* If I hadn't been wearing clothes, we'd both see the flush covering me, head to toe. Every redhead's bane.

The handsome Norse-godlike creature who stood there, amusement clear in his face, had butterflies hitting my stomach in full migration. His absolutely lickable lips curled up on one side, and his eyes were crinkled at the corners. And now that I had licking on the mind, really, his whole body looked as lickable as a giant lollipop of male proportions.

Why was I pooling drool in my mouth instead of forming words? Only the Goddess would know, but words continued to fail me. *Those bastards!* I needed some goddamn words. Words that didn't amount to cussing at my customer. I tried, again, to remind myself that I had a business to run, but geez, his way-taller-than-me muscular build—*Was he six feet?*—had shut my brain right down.

So I did the only thing I could do.

Absolutely nothing.

Priceless.

I just stood there gaping. Gaping and watching as his hazel—of course, they had to be hazel—eyes crinkled even more. Since I had nothing better to do with my brain cells in hibernation, I pondered the universe. More specifically why the universe saw fit to throw gods in the way of mere mortals and then, insult to injury, wrap all that perfection in a sexy business suit of dark gray, with a crisp white shirt unbuttoned at his throat. That was just downright mean. I was calling foul!

With my search for words being absolutely useless, I remembered I still had my damn keys to get, so I bent down to grab them because, why not?

His groan above alerted me to my miscalculation. You see, we'd still been standing relatively close together when I reached down. With that brilliant move, I found my head in dangerous proximity to his groin. His now slightly bulging groin. Or was that my imagination?

It took a moment, because it really was a lovely view, but I came back to my senses. I'd been caught ogling his groin. *Yikes!* I averted my eyes and swiftly grabbed for the slippery-as-fuck keys. That's when I heard Kevin, who must have come in from the kitchen, say, "Oh honey. If you want to do that, you may want to turn that sign back to closed. I don't blame you though. Welcome to The Frisky Bean. Coffee? Tea? Me? Please tell me it's me."

All I wanted was for the ground to open and swallow me whole. Thinking about opening and swallowing, with my head where it was, proved a really bad idea that left me damp and dying all at once. I finally had the keys in my grasp and somehow made it to a standing position without falling over and glared at Kevin. Finding my voice—hallelujah— I growled out, "Kevin Dwayne Johnson! That is *not* an appropriate way to greet a customer!"

Of course, neither was yours. Whatever.

I turned towards said customer only to find him still silently sporting a sexy-as-sin grin. His eyes, though... *Damn*, his eyes held a warm heat I was pretty sure was directed my way, and my insides liquified. I thought I heard Kevin snort and mumble under his breath, "Pot, kettle, black, sister." Then there was silence as the door to the kitchen swooshed and I assumed Kevin left.

"I...am...so...incredibly...sorry...for everything that has happened in the last few minutes. Can we please pretend none of this ever happened? None of it. Ever."

ABOUT THE AUTHOR

Michelle Mars has an unhealthy obsession with coffee, caramel, and funny t-shirts. This single mom of two amazing, kind, and creative dragons/children has naturally purple hair and loves nothing more than talking books, kids, and living your best life. She enjoys reading romance, traveling, and writing stories that make her readers laugh, sweat, and swoon.

Author of the steamy, paranormal, sci-fi, romcom Love Wars Series; Moving Jack, Adoring Alexis, Chasing Rory, Embracing Irina, and Claiming Jill out now. Loving Will is later this year.

And, the contemporary romcom series, The Frisky Bean; Frisky Intentions, the short story prequel, Frisky Connections, and Frisky Collections Volume 1, Frisky and Queer out now. Frisky Business is coming soon.

Michelle's truth: Humor is a turn-on!

For updates go to www.michellemars.com and register to her newsletter.

facebook.com/michellemarsbooks

x.com/MichelleMarsHEA

instagram.com/michellemarsbooks

amazon.com/stores/Michelle-Mars/author/B07WZX3X97

bookbub.com/profile/michelle-mars

tiktok.com/@authormichellemars

Frisky Connections

Frisky Intentions

<u>Other Work:</u>

Moving Jack, Love Wars Book 1

You can buy the above cover in print signed by me from my website www. michellemars.com.

Chasing Rory, Love Wars Book 2

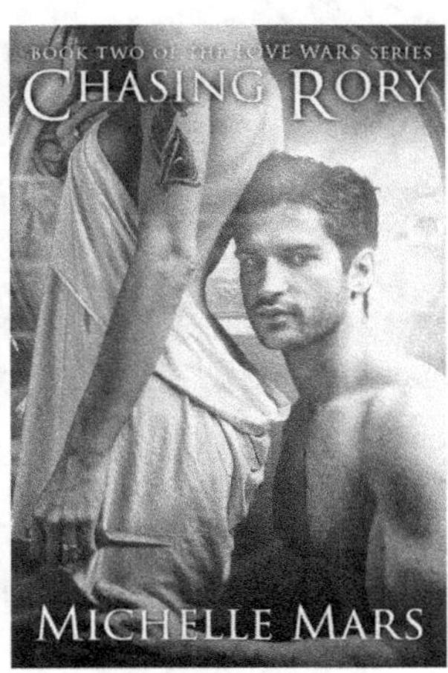

You can buy the above cover in print signed by me from my website www. michellemars.com.

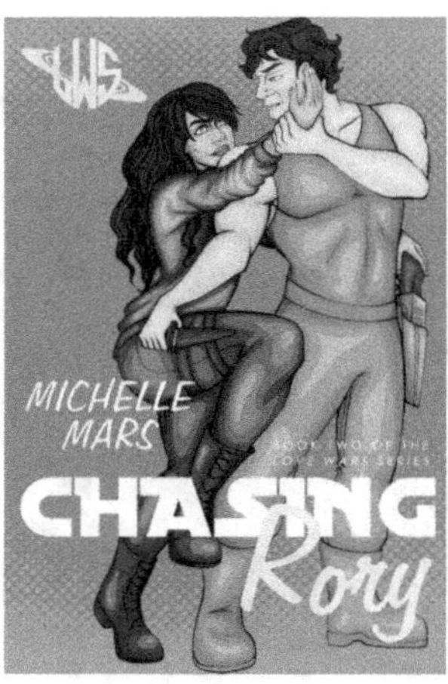

Embracing Irina, Love Wars Book 0.5 Prequel

You can buy the above cover in print signed by me from my website www.
michellemars.com.

Claiming Jill, Love Wars Book 3

You can buy the above cover in print signed by me from my website www. michellemars.com.

MICHELLE MARS
CLAIMING Jill
BOOK THREE OF THE LOVE WARS SERIES

www.ingramcontent.com/pod-product-compliance
Lightning Source LLC
Chambersburg PA
CBHW070515200726

48293CB00007B/2541